A Brass Anchor
Inn Christmas

Jennifer Faye

Lazy Dazy Press

Published by Lazy Dazy Press

Editor: Lia Fairchild

Contents

In memory of Writer Kitty

I can't believe our journey together has come to an end.
This is the last book we wrote together. It will always be special to me.
I hope I made you proud.
You were the best writing buddy and you are missed every day.
Thank you for letting me be your human.
Love you forever...

About this book...

THIS SNOWY **C**HRISTMAS, THERE'S a new matchmaker on Bluestar Island, and she's working on Project: Mistletoe...

Carol Carmichael operates the refresh décor service at Turner Home Furnishings, but business has recently dropped off, putting her job in jeopardy. Misfortune strikes the island, and Bluestar's annual ten-day Christmas celebration is moved to the new ballroom at the Brass Anchor Inn. Carol is asked to decorate the ballroom for the festivities. Could the high visibility of this project be exactly what she needs to keep her job? There's just one catch...working at the inn will put her in direct contact with the man who broke her heart.

Hotel manager Harvey Coleman is not feeling the holiday spirit. A health scare has him pulling back from life and those who care about him. But when Carol arrives at the inn, she turns his frown upside down with her sunny smiles. There's no way she'll give him a second chance...even if he wants one.

As Christmas approaches, a bit of matchmaking keeps their lives intertwined. Will the spirit of the season heal their hearts and a sprig of mistletoe give their love a second chance?

Includes a recipe for Carol's Chai Spice Cookies!

Bluestar Island series:

Book 1: Love Blooms

Book 2: Harvest Dance

Book 3: A Lighthouse Café Christmas

Book 4: Rising Star

Book 5: Summer by the Beach

Book 6: Brass Anchor Inn

Book 7: Summer Refresh

Book 8: A Seaside Bookshop Christmas

Book 9: A Lighthouse Snapshot

Book 10: Inheriting Her Island House

Book 11: A Brass Anchor Inn Christmas

Book 12: Race to the Beach

Prologue

December 9th

S HE HAD A PLAN.

But she needed a little help.

Josie Turner stepped up to the checkout counter of the Seaside Bookshop. It was owned by Melinda Coleman, who was not only a close friend but also her sister-in-law. The countertop was decorated with red garland and white twinkle lights. On one end stood the cash register, and on the other end was a small Christmas tree decked out with miniature ornaments. Josie leaned in closer to get a better look at one particular ornament: a penguin with a candy cane. It was so cute.

This all just went to prove what she already knew—she lacked the decorating gene. Sure, the inn was decorated, but it was the same old decorations they used year after year. There was nothing special to make anyone *ooh* and *aah* over. Luckily, the guests seemed content with her efforts.

There was no one there. "Melinda?"

"I'll be right there." Melinda's voice came from the back of the bookshop.

"Okay. No rush." Josie took the moment to look around the bookshop.

Her friend definitely had a knack for decorating. The whole bookshop exuded the holiday spirit. She inhaled and got the slightest whiff of evergreen from the skinny Christmas tree in the reading area. A smile pulled at the corners of her lips.

"Sorry about that." Melinda Coleman stepped out from the back room. Her abdomen was rounded with her first baby. "I was finishing inventorying the latest shipment of books." She paused as she looked at Josie. "Is everything all right?"

"Yes… Um… No." Josie sighed. "I don't know."

Melinda's brows drew together. "It sounds like this conversation would be best held with a warm drink in hand." She stepped out from behind the counter and headed over to the area for customers to relax and read a book. There were a couple of other people there. One young man appeared completely immersed in the book he was reading, and the other woman had in earbuds as she typed on her laptop. Neither paid them any attention.

"How are you and the baby doing?" Josie asked.

"Good. I just had a doctor's appointment, and I was told everything is right on schedule."

"That's great. In no time at all, I'll be babysitting for you."

Melinda smiled as she moved to the coffee station. "What would you like? I can offer you coffee? Tea? Or hot chocolate?"

"Considering it's snowing outside and I had coffee not so long ago, I'll go with the hot chocolate."

Once they had their drinks, they moved to a corner table. Melinda used a swizzle stick with a snowman at the top to stir her herbal tea. "What's going on with you? I haven't seen you much lately."

Josie took a sip of the creamy, rich chocolate. She licked her lips. "Sorry. I've just been focused on getting ready for the holidays. By the way, you did an amazing job decorating this place."

"Thank you, but I have a feeling you didn't stop by just to talk about my holiday decorations." Melinda knew her so well.

Josie wasn't sure where to start with this conversation. She didn't want her friend to think she was being meddlesome, even if that was exactly what she was about to do. But she couldn't stand by without doing something to bring these two people together.

Josie sipped at the hot chocolate with extra mini marshmallows. She licked the froth from her lips. "How do you think your father is doing?"

Melinda shrugged. "Pretty good. He's watching what he eats, taking his meds and going for walks. Why?"

Josie suddenly had the feeling this was a bad idea—a terrible idea. After all, what did she know about matchmaking? Still, the idea niggled at the back of her mind.

Melinda leaned forward. "Now you're starting to worry me. Is there something I should know?"

Josie shook her head. "It's nothing to worry about."

"And yet I'm worried. So, please tell me."

Josie inhaled a deep breath and released it. "Is he dating anyone?"

"No. Ever since my mother died, he's said that part of his life is over. I tried to get him back out there, but he refuses."

Josie worried the inside of her lip as she tried to decide what to tell her friend. "Before his heart attack, he found someone he was interested in."

"I don't know." Melinda looked skeptical.

"He was asking me dating advice."

Melinda's eyes widened. "No way! Who?"

"My aunt. He seemed really nervous. And I think they started dating, but then his heart attack happened. I don't think they're still seeing each other."

"I knew they were friends, but I didn't know it was more than that." Melinda shrugged. "Maybe it just didn't work out."

"I thought so at first, but I saw them the other day at the Lighthouse Cafe."

"So, they're seeing each other again?"

"By the awkwardness and distance between them, I don't think so. There was a lot of tension between them."

Melinda was quiet for a moment as she sipped her tea. "Why are you talking to me about this instead of your aunt?"

"Because I think those two have a lot of unfinished business." It wasn't until the words crossed her lips that she realized it might not have been the right thing to say to her friend. She didn't know how Melinda felt about her father getting serious with anyone since her mother passed away. So, she decided to amend her response. "I just think they deserve a chance to see if they belong together. Right now, I think they're finding excuses to stay apart."

Melinda remained silent. Her brow crinkled, as though she were giving this idea some thought. Before she could respond, the bell above the front door jingled. Time was running out to convince her friend to help her with this bit of holiday matchmaking.

"Think about it," Josie said. "They're around the same age. They both know what it's like to lose a spouse. And they both seem lonely."

"I don't know," Melinda said. "What if this is a mistake? I don't want my dad to get hurt."

"And I don't want my aunt to get hurt, but I'm telling you that there's something between them."

Melinda glanced over as more people entered the bookshop. "I don't have much more time to talk. What do you have in mind?"

Josie leaned forward and lowered her voice. "Here's what I think we should do..."

CHAPTER ONE

Two days later / Fourteen days before Christmas

*W*EE-OOW. *WEE-OOW.*

Sirens had been going off all night and into the morning.

The wind howled while sleet clicked against the windows.

Carol Carmichael let out a yawn as she moved to her apartment window. Even though it was almost eight in the morning, the sky was still a dark gray. A winter storm had hovered over the island most of the night.

According to the online weather report, it should pass by noon. Another gust of wind rattled the windows. Noon couldn't come fast enough.

Buzz.

She reached for her phone and was surprised to find the caller was Kent Turner, her nephew and boss at Turner Home Furnishings. She pressed the phone to her ear. "Hey, Kent. Everything okay?"

"This storm is bad. My place is good and so is my parents', but there are a lot of people that didn't fare so well. I just called to let you know we're not going to open the store today. I'm out on a call with the fire department, helping with the clean-up. Thankfully, there have been no major injuries with this storm."

"I'll cook some food for the volunteers and anyone else who needs a hot meal. Is there anything else I can do?" She knew that was one of the great things about living on Bluestar Island: in times of need, the residents came together to help each other.

"That sounds like plenty. I think people are gathering at the church."

"Okay. I'll be there shortly. And, Kent, be careful out there."

"I will. You too."

Carol set aside her phone and rushed to the kitchen cabinets. She threw them open, not sure what supplies she had on hand. Thankfully, she'd gone to the market earlier that week, so there was some food. She pulled out boxes and cans.

Even though she was in her late fifties, she didn't have a family of her own. So, she didn't have an excuse to cook very often. She missed spending time in the kitchen.

A few hours later, Carol had a macaroni and cheese casserole, baked rigatoni, and a tray of brownies. She made numerous trips to her golf cart to get everything loaded. After moving to Bluestar, it had taken her a long time to get used to no cars being allowed on the island. Instead, everyone commuted via golf carts, bikes, or by walking.

Luckily, the carts on the island came with doors and heaters. In fact, they not only came in numerous colors, but they also had many options available from upholstery to two or four doors. She had a four-door model to allow for hauling supplies for her job.

With all of the food secured in the backseat, she set off for the church. It had become a community hub while the community center was now acting as the temporary medical center until the construction of the new hospital was completed. In fact, they'd moved a number of the upcoming Christmas events to the church's fellowship room.

Driving across town took much longer than she expected. The windshield wipers ran the whole time. Between the continued sleet and the tree limbs on the roadway, it was slow going. And in a couple of places, the power lines were down, causing traffic to turn around and take a detour.

Bluestar was a mess, but it didn't stop people from getting out to lend a helping hand. People were bundled up against the winter weather. Some held chainsaws to cut up the debris. Others were helping to direct traffic around the hazards.

On her way to the church, Carol ended up going past the site of the new hospital. They had the red brick exterior constructed. The windows had been installed, and the roof was in place.

At the moment, it was dark inside, but she knew when the storm moved on, the workers would be back at it. They were supposed to be working on the interior of the hospital during the winter months. The building was huge, at least in Bluestar terms.

When she approached the intersection to turn onto the street where the church was located, she found flashing red lights. *Oh no.* The road was blocked off with emergency services yellow saw horses.

She kept going until she found the first available parking spot so she wouldn't have to carry the food very far. When she got out, she yanked up the hood on her red coat to help protect her from the bits of ice raining down on the island.

With the macaroni and cheese in hand, she set off back toward the church. It wasn't the easiest to walk. The sidewalks were caked with snow and ice. Carol slipped a couple of times but was able to regain her balance before falling. She was grateful the island didn't get these sorts of storms very often.

Even on foot, she couldn't get close to the church. The building was roped off with yellow caution tape. She stopped and stared up at the building.

She gasped at the severe damage. A giant tree had fallen into the church. A large portion of the roof had been destroyed. *Oh my!* She couldn't even imagine the extent of the damage to the interior.

After a moment, she turned away from the disheartening sight. She approached one of her nephews, Owen. He was the youngest of the

Turner siblings. He looked so grown up in his firefighter's uniform and helmet. *My how time passed so quickly.* It seemed like just yesterday when he was a teenager tinkering around in his parents' garage, working on a boat motor.

When he glanced in her direction, a smile lifted the corners of his mouth. She smiled back. Even though it was a small town, they didn't see each other that much, other than the family dinners at her sister's house.

She stopped next to him and gestured toward the church. "Was anyone hurt?"

He shook his head. "Luckily there was no one in there."

"That's good news. Do you know where people are taking food?"

"Try the fire station." He gave her a concerned look. "Is everything okay with you?"

She nodded. Owen had always been a sweet boy when he was younger. Quieter than his older brothers. Something told her he was always lost in his imagination. It was what made him so great at writing those digital games that so many people were so crazy about.

"You shouldn't be out in this ice." His voice held a note of concern.

"I'll head home just as soon as I drop off the food."

Someone called out to Owen and he had to go.

She took one more look at the church. It was such a shocking sight. She hoped everyone on the island was safe.

ell

They hadn't had a bad storm like this in years.

Harvey Coleman stood by the door of the firehouse and stared out at the winter storm. Fire Chief Ethan Walker redirected him there after finding the church in ruins. When he'd arrived, there hadn't been anyone around to set things up.

Luckily, he knew his way around the firehouse, as he used to be a firefighter. It had been many years ago. Most of the men on the island had volunteered at one point in their life. In a lot of families, it was a tradition. So, it wasn't hard for him to find what he needed to transform the bays of the firehouse into a warming station. It would provide refuge for those without power and a dining hall for anyone who needed a hot meal, especially the hardworking volunteers.

Ethan told him to take advantage of the space and he did. There was space to eat and places to rest. When the trucks eventually returned from what appeared to be a long day of helping the community, they'd park outside.

No sooner had he set up some cots and the folding tables than the food started to arrive. He walked over to the buffet to rearrange the many dishes to make room for additional food that would inevitably show up.

As was common for Bluestar, there was more than enough food. No matter how he arranged the various dishes, there just wasn't room for much more. If more food was delivered, he'd need to set up yet another table.

No sooner had the thought crossed his mind than the door opened. A whoosh of frigid air rushed inside. He turned his head to see Carol making her way inside. He paused. She was wearing a ruby-red coat and a snow-white scarf over her head. He'd always liked that coat on her. It made her look like a glamorous movie star. When she lowered the hood, he noticed her cheeks and nose were pink from the cold air. She still looked beautiful.

His first instinct was to rush to her side, but he hesitated. It was best he didn't make a big deal out of her presence. She hadn't taken it well when he'd ended things between them, not that he could blame her.

What is she doing out in this winter storm? With the ice and wind, it wasn't safe being out and about.

It was only then that he noticed she was holding a large casserole dish. *And yet more food.* He was going to have to contact his daughter, Melinda, and have her post on the community social media that there was food for everyone.

Still, the dish looked heavy for her. It would be reasonable that he would assist her. After all, he would lend a hand to anyone else.

The last time they'd spoken, it hadn't gone well. But with the island being under a state of emergency, they needed to set aside their problems. This wasn't about them. This was about helping their friends and neighbors.

In measured steps, he made his way to the doorway. In his friendliest tone, he said, "Let me take that for you."

Carol hesitated. "Oh. Uh... Sure." She relinquished the dish. "I need to get more out of my cart."

More? "I can get it for you."

He carried the casserole dish that smelled of tomatoes, garlic, and oregano over to the table. His mouth watered. The one thing he remembered about Carol was that she was a talented cook. He missed her cooking. It was only one of the many things he missed about her.

He halted his meandering thoughts as he placed the dish in the only open spot on the table. "I'll go get the other food, and then I'll set up another table."

Her eyes widened when she saw the tables. "It looks like you have a lot of food."

He nodded. "The food keeps coming."

Worry lines creased between her brows. "Maybe I shouldn't have brought this."

He didn't want her to feel that her efforts weren't appreciated. "It's almost lunchtime. I'm sure the people will descend upon here any time now with huge appetites."

"Maybe you're right." She continued to stare at the various dishes. "Oh. And you have coffee too."

He nodded. "I found a couple of large coffee makers in the kitchen. I thought people would need the warmth and caffeine. It's going to be a long day." He pointed over his shoulder to the refreshment table. "Help yourself. I'll just go get the other dish."

"Actually, there are two more dishes. The mac-n-cheese is in a slow cooker to keep it warm, and then there's a couple of batches of brownies."

He turned and headed outside. It wasn't so long ago that he'd be out there cutting up fallen trees and hauling away the debris. After his heart attack, he left the heavy lifting to the younger guys. These days he was more cautious and tended to the food for the people who were dealing with the storm debris.

When he returned, he noticed that Carol was unusually quiet. He wasn't sure what to say to break the awkward silence or if he should even try. When she at last asked if there was anything she could do, he gently turned down her offer. She made a hasty exit. He wanted to ask her to stick around. She could help him with the food, but he knew it wasn't a good idea. Nothing good would come of them spending too much time together—even if he wished their circumstances could be different.

Chapter Two

Thirteen days before Christmas

"WHITE CHRISTMAS" PLAYED SOFTLY on the speaker system.

This was the best time of the year.

Thursday morning, Carol sat in her office at Turner Home Furnishings and hummed along with the song. Her computer was on, and she was staring at her calendar or rather worrying about its emptiness. Business had started to dwindle off before Thanksgiving. Now her workload was practically non-existent, except for a few small jobs here and there. And she was worried.

After her husband of more than thirty years passed on, she'd moved from Ohio to Bluestar Island to be closer to some of her family. She thought it would help fill the gaping hole in her heart. And it had in a way. But now as she rebuilt her life, she felt as though she were still missing something. Maybe she needed to adopt a cat.

Her contemplation was interrupted by a knock at her office door. She glanced up to see her beautiful niece standing there. "Hey, Josie. What brings you by?"

Josie smiled at her aunt as she moved toward one of the two chairs in front of Carol's desk. She sat down. "I don't know if you heard, but since the church was damaged during the storm, the town is in need of a new place to hold some of the holiday festivities."

Carol nodded her head. "I saw the church. It's just awful what happened. I don't know what the town's going to do for the holidays but there's no way they can use the church."

"Agreed. And that's why the mayor approached me about hosting some of the events at the inn. However, in order to do that, I'm going to need your help." Josie's eyes pleaded with her.

"You know I'm always here to help you." The response was automatic, and it wasn't until it was spoken that she felt as though she should have gotten all of the details before volunteering herself. "What exactly do you have in mind?"

"Don't look so worried." Josie sent her a reassuring smile. "This is within your area of expertise."

Carol was still hesitant. "And what would that be?"

"I was hoping you could work some of your magic and turn the inn into some sort of Christmas wonderland."

"But why? You've already done a beautiful job decorating the place."

Josie waved away the compliment. "I do the same thing every year, just like the prior owner. Sandra Barton was wonderful, but she got stuck in a rut, doing the same things year after year. I don't want that to happen to me. I want to step it up this year—make it extra special."

"And you think I can do that?"

Josie nodded. "I do."

The idea of decorating the inn sounded like a fun, yet challenging project. An image of the lobby flashed in her mind. There were so many possibilities.

In the next breath, reality came crashing in on her. The inn was Harvey's domain. He had been the manager for years. She was certain he wouldn't appreciate her presence. And she wasn't so sure she wanted to endure his company either. After all, he'd dumped her. It had been so abrupt that she hadn't even seen it coming.

It was best she kept her distance. She just hoped her niece would understand. "I'm sorry, Josie, but I don't think I can do something like that in such a short amount of time."

Josie looked crestfallen. "Are you sure? I know this is short notice, but I can pay you extra."

She'd give Josie an *A* for effort. "How does Lane feel about this?"

Lane was Josie's business partner plus they were newlyweds. Carol's only hope of getting out of this tactfully was if Lane was opposed to her decorating the inn. But would he even care?

Josie momentarily hesitated, as though surprised by the question. "Well, I didn't exactly run it past him. He's been dealing with some business problems. And I didn't want to lay this on him too."

"So, what you're saying is that taking on the responsibility for hosting the holiday festivities is all on you?"

Josie nodded. "Now you understand. The town has been through a lot this year, and I just want to give them a place where they can come and celebrate together."

Carol was still adjusting to just how close-knit this town was. It was like one great big family that squabbled but always came together when one of them was in need. It was something very special and rare.

Maybe she could help her niece without running into Harvey very much. After all, it wasn't like they would have to talk, much less work together. In fact, maybe she could arrange her work schedule at the inn to miss him as much as possible.

"Please say you'll do it." Josie's eyes pleaded with her.

How could she resist her? It was just like when Josie was a little girl and they would go shopping. Josie would see a toy that she just had to have. Carol was always a softie and would get it for her while Josie's mother would just shake her head. It appeared she was still a pushover.

"Okay, Josie. I'll do a holiday refresh at the inn. Do you have anything special in mind?"

"As a matter of fact, I do." She reached into her over-sized purse and pulled out a digital tablet. "I made some notes..."

CHAPTER THREE

Twelve days before Christmas

THIS USED TO BE his favorite time of the year...

The following morning, Harvey stood at the reception desk at the Brass Anchor Inn. Normally, he wore a Santa hat to go with his white mustache and beard. The littles would often mistake him for Santa. He didn't mind playing into the fantasy. He'd even perfected his *ho-ho-ho*.

But this year, he couldn't muster up the enthusiasm to wear the red plush hat much less inquire what the children wanted for Christmas. He'd lost his holiday spirit. He blamed it on his heart attack. Coming that close to dying had profoundly changed him.

This was his second Christmas since he'd come way too close to meeting his maker and the pep in his step still hadn't come back. Having just turned sixty-one, he decided to just take it easy this Christmas and let the holiday pass by him without any fanfare. As soon as the thought came to him, he realized it wouldn't be that easy since the inn was hosting a few of the town's annual holiday events.

The door to the inn's lobby opened. He straightened his shoulders and plastered on his usual smile. "Welcome to the Brass Anchor Inn."

When the woman lifted her head, the smile instantly vanished from his face. *Carol? What is she doing here?*

She walked right up to the reception desk like she owned the place. She didn't smile. "Hello, Harvey."

"What are you..." He stopped himself. That was not the way the inn's manager should react. He swallowed hard. "How may I help you?"

She arched a brow. "How unlike you to be out of the loop." She hesitated as though deciding whether or not to inform him. "I'm here to meet with Josie. She's hired me to give the inn a holiday refresh."

His mouth opened but then wordlessly closed. What was he supposed to do with this information?

He didn't want Carol at the inn—to see her at every turn. *No. This has to be a mistake.* Perhaps some sort of joke. But Carol wasn't laughing.

His only hope was that she wouldn't be there for long. After all, how much time could it possibly take to put up a few decorations. Speaking of which, Josie had already put up decorations. Why would she want more?

And then he recalled the mayor's impromptu visit the other day. He must have gotten Josie worked up about the townspeople visiting the inn. Harvey could understand that. Though he didn't think Josie had a thing to worry about. The inn was stately and beautiful. Anyone would tell her that.

As for Carol, it was best to keep his distance. He called Josie and let her know Carol had arrived for their meeting. Josie informed him that she would be there in a moment.

After he delivered the message to Carol, she made no motion to move to one of the chairs. Unable to ignore her closeness and how she made his pulse race, he said, "I, uh...need to go check on something." When Carol arched a brow, he said, "Room 112 is having problems with the plumbing." It was the truth.

This time he didn't wait for a reaction as he turned and strode off. He knew he needed to monitor the front desk. He would only be gone a moment—long enough for him to gather himself, and hopefully, long enough for Carol to move on.

Could this day get any worse? He realized the danger of tempting fate, especially when it was only eight thirty in the morning. It left a lot of hours in which life could go sideways.

He'd barely taken a few steps down the hallway when he heard, "Harvey, there you are." Josie headed toward him. "I meant to speak with you."

So, now she was going to explain what Carol was doing in the lobby. His only question was how long was this decorating going to take?

Before he could vocalize the words, she said, "If you're going to check on room 112, you don't have to." She smiled at him. "Problem solved."

"Oh." His shoulders slumped. This meant he had to go back to the lobby, and Carol was still there. And the problem wasn't that he didn't like her. In fact, the problem was quite the opposite. He liked her too much. But he'd burned that bridge to the ground.

Josie studied his face. "You don't look happy. Is everything all right?"

There wasn't a chance he was going to tell her he was trying to avoid Carol. Instead, he nodded. "Everything is fine."

Jingle. Jingle.

It was the bell in the lobby. A guest had arrived. Harvey hesitated.

"Harvey?" Josie gave him a concerned look. "Are you sure you're feeling all right? If you need to go home early, I can cover for you."

He shook his head. Josie was almost like another daughter to him. He didn't want her worrying over him. "I'm fine. But thank you for caring."

And with that he walked away. When he stepped into the lobby, he immediately noticed an older couple at the reception desk. His gaze moved beyond them and searched for Carol. When he didn't immediately notice her, he breathed a sigh of relief.

He stepped behind the desk. "How may I help you?"

For the next few minutes, he explained to them some of the places they should visit on the island. Once the guests set off to explore the island, he checked the register to see how many new guests they were expecting that day.

As his gaze scanned down over the digital register, he heard a thud or a thunk. It sounded like something had fallen, but what could it be? He scanned the lobby but didn't see anything amiss. It must have been some ice falling from the roof. He shrugged it off and focused back on the computer screen.

Thunk!

This time he noticed the sound wasn't coming from outside. He stepped out from behind the desk. He stopped in the middle of the lobby and turned in a circle, scanning the room. Surely some creature hadn't sneaked in the door.

Harvey stared down at the floor as he made his way around the perimeter of the room.

Thunk.

There it was again. It was coming from the other side of the room. He moved toward the display cases that held various articles of Bluestar's history.

He rushed around the corner and collided with someone. He instinctively reached out, bracing the other person's shoulders with his hands. When he regained his balance and lifted his head, his gaze was met with the most stunning blue eyes. It was Carol. His heart thudded in his chest.

When he found himself staring into her mesmerizing eyes a moment too long, he averted his gaze. Certain she was once again steady on her feet, he released his hold and stepped back.

He struggled to gather himself. This was as close as he'd been to her since his heart attack—since he thought his life was over. He didn't realize how much he missed her. His fingers tingled to reach out and pull her close again.

However, his medical scare had been a wakeup call for him. His father had died young from a heart attack. And he was pretty certain his grandfather had died before his time from a heart attack. It seemed history was about to repeat itself. And he wouldn't put Carol through the misery like he'd gone through when he'd lost his wife and like Carol had suffered when she lost her husband. It was best to just keep his distance. If only Carol would respect his decision and keep her distance.

He lifted his gaze to meet hers. She didn't smile at him nor did she frown. "Hello again."

"What are you doing over here?"

Her brows gathered as confusion shone in her eyes. "I thought we already discussed this."

His back teeth ground together. Why was she making this difficult? She knew what he meant. "What are you still doing here?"

"Oh. While I was waiting for Josie, I decided to take some measurements so I could work up a sketch."

Her explanation took the steam out of his frustration. "And what was the thunking sound I heard?"

"Oh. That was me." She sent him an innocent smile. "I was checking to see if these display cases could be moved."

"No."

"Excuse me?"

"No, they can't be moved. You'll have to work around them."

She arched a brow. "Are you now in charge of the Christmas display?"

"What?" That would mean working with her. And that wasn't going to happen. "No, of course not. It's just that these cases hold a lot of the island's history. A lot of the content is fragile. Besides, it would be a lot of work to move them."

"I see." She jotted something in the notebook.

He wanted to ask what she was writing, but he held back his words. "I need to get back to work."

"So do I." When he turned away, she said, "Harvey, I don't know what I did to get on your bad side, but I'd like to think we could still co-exist in the same space."

Co-exist? It was going to be a balancing act to hold her at an arm's length and still "co-exist" with her. Maybe he was being too harsh in his effort to keep a safe distance between them. It had never been his intention to be hostile.

With a sigh, he said, "We can co-exist."

"Oh, good." She sent him a tentative smile. "I was thinking you were going to hate me forever."

"Hate?" The word popped out of his mouth before he could stop it. "I never hated you."

Jingle. Jingle.

Thank goodness. Before this conversation could get even more uncomfortable, he said, "I have to get back to work." And yet, he hesitated. "Seriously, if I were you, I would consider a plan where these cases don't have to be moved. They are very heavy."

She nodded. "I think you're right."

And then he returned to the front desk. He found himself periodically glancing in Carol's direction. He assured himself it was just part of his job to make sure she didn't disturb any of the displays. His interest had absolutely nothing to do with wanting to catch a glimpse of her. Because he had no business staring at that beautiful woman—no business at all. That part of his life was over.

CHAPTER FOUR

Eleven days before Christmas

M AYBE THIS WASN'T SUCH a good idea after all.

Melinda Coleman made her way out of the Seaside Bookshop. Josie had messaged her and asked if they could meet for coffee at the Lighthouse Cafe. Her assistant would watch over the bookshop while she was gone. She snuggled deeper into her coat. Snowflakes danced and twirled in the sky. All the while, she wondered what she'd gotten herself into by agreeing to this matchmaking scheme.

Last evening, when she'd dropped off some food for her father, he'd been quieter than normal. Something had been bothering him. The thought that she might be indirectly responsible for whatever was troubling him didn't sit well with her.

Being seven months pregnant, she carefully navigated her way along the recently shoveled sidewalk. Thankfully, most of the ice from the storm the other day had melted. She shared greetings with those she passed. Life was getting back to normal.

She knew this meeting with Josie was about more than coffee. She'd been having misgivings about this matchmaking idea ever since Josie brought it up. And yet she hadn't tried to stop Josie, because she knew her father wasn't happy. She got the feeling he was lonely.

She tried to spend as much time with him as she could but between running the bookshop and spending time with her new family, it didn't leave much time. Plus, this pregnancy had her growing tired quickly.

Her father needed someone else in his life. But was matchmaking the right move? She worried her father would be so upset with her if he ever learned what they were up to.

But if Josie was right and there was something unresolved between him and Carol, maybe they just needed a little nudge back toward each other. After all, she wanted to see her father happy again. Her mother had been gone for many years, and she didn't believe her mother would want her father to be alone the rest of his life.

At the café, she reached out a gloved hand and pulled open the door. She passed by the community bulletin board, where people posted all sorts of things from items for sale to help wanted. Today, the only thing Melinda needed was some sort of assurance that she wasn't making a mistake with this matchmaking scheme.

With it being mid-morning, there weren't a lot of people in the restaurant. She quickly scanned the dining room, barely noticing the beach murals painted on the walls. Her gaze momentarily paused on the miniature Christmas tree situated on the counter at the back of the restaurant. As a little girl, she'd always marveled over the itsy-bitsy ornaments on the tree. They were so cute.

Not having time to reminisce, she glanced at the whitewashed wood tables and chairs. She noticed how every tabletop had the usual black and white lighthouse ornament with a little wreath affixed to it. As her gaze continued around the room, she at last spotted Josie in a corner booth.

"How's it going?" Melinda sat across from Josie, who had already ordered drinks for the both of them as there was a cup of herbal tea waiting for her.

While "Jingle Bell Rock" softly played over the sound system, Josie added some sweetener to her coffee and a dose of milk before giving it a swirl. "I think this plan is going to be more work than I anticipated."

"That's why I have an idea." If she was going to take part in this, she might as well contribute to the effort.

Josie's face lit up. "Do tell..."

Melinda reached into her backpack purse and pulled out a book. She slid it across the table to Josie. "I just gave a copy of this cozy mystery to my father. Perhaps you could give this copy to Carol."

Josie picked up the book and turned it over to glance at the back cover copy. "I don't even know if she likes to read."

"She likes to read," Melinda said confidently. She'd seen Carol in the bookshop numerous times over the past couple of years since she moved to the island.

Josie blinked. "Oh, okay. But why couldn't you give it to her?"

"Because I just gave a copy to my father. It would seem a little suspicious if I gave them both a copy."

Josie paused. "I suppose so. But why the book?"

"Why not a book?" Melinda's gaze searched hers. "Maybe they just need to find something in common to talk about. What could be better than a book?"

Josie looked unconvinced. "I don't know. Won't they find it suspicious that they are reading the same book?"

"I made sure it's a new release. Lots of people will be reading it."

Josie took a sip of coffee. "What do I say when I give her the book?"

"I... I don't know." She wasn't very good at this matchmaking stuff. When Josie frowned, Melinda said, "Maybe tell her you found it." When Josie didn't say anything, Melinda felt as though she needed to keep going. "Maybe tell her you found it in a guest room." The more she thought about it, the more she liked the idea. "Yes, tell her you found it. One of the guests forgot it. When you reached out to them, they said to give it to someone. And you thought of her."

"Wow. That's good. I'll do it."

Melinda thought about mentioning her father's melancholy mood, but she hesitated. She didn't want Josie to take it as a sign that they needed to ramp up their matchmaking. Instead, they talked about the upcoming Christmas festivities. Josie told her how the inn had been selected to play host for a lot of the activities. Melinda acted surprised and pleased at the news, but the truth was that she'd heard about it a while ago from Agnes Dewey, who heard it from someone else in the gossip chain. Nothing was a secret for long on the island.

Melinda drank her tea before checking the time. "I need to get back to the shop. Do you need anything else?"

Josie shook her head. Then she whispered, "Just so you know, I'm sending them on a mission."

Alarm bells rang in Melinda's mind. Part of her wanted to walk away and pretend she hadn't heard her, but the responsible part had her asking, "What sort of mission?"

"A Christmas one."

"Josie, you don't want to push them too hard. This could blow up in both of our faces. Isn't it enough that you have your aunt working at the inn?"

Josie waved off her worry. "I don't think you comprehend just how stubborn these two can be."

That was true. Her father could be more stubborn than an old mule. "What is this Christmas mission you have in mind?"

Josie's phone rang. She retrieved it from her purse. "I'm sorry. I need to grab this. It's Lane and he had to fly to California this week."

"Okay. You can fill me in later." Melinda got up and headed for the door.

She still wasn't sure about this matchmaking thing, but she felt as though they were in so deep now that they might as well see how it worked out. Just then she felt a swift kick from the baby. She wondered if they were trying to kick some sense into her.

She rubbed the spot where the baby continued to kick. "It's okay, little one. Everything will work out."

She hoped...

Only four days until the first festive event at the inn...

Carol's stomach shivered with nerves. She was having second thoughts about agreeing to this holiday refresh. When she'd visited the inn the day before, Josie had shown her the rooms she wanted decorated. They'd talked about how elaborate Josie wanted the decorating to be, which was quite extensive.

Carol felt so much pressure to get this project right. If the decorations weren't spectacular, it would do nothing to increase her bookings in the New Year. But it couldn't be too far over the top, because in the end this was still a small town.

The balance of glam and traditional had to be just right.

And the truth was that she needed this job more than she'd let on to her family. They thought she was set for retirement. Nothing could be further from the truth. Her husband's medical bills wiped out most of their savings. Not that she begrudged spending the money. If she had to do it all over again, she would have made the exact same choices. They were able to spend almost an extra year together because of the treatments. That time was worth all of the money in the world.

Now, she had to start over. It wasn't always easy, but she was learning that she was stronger than she ever imagined. Since moving to the island, she found she had a renewed sense of energy and drive. She'd worked late into the night on sketches of her visions for a Brass Anchor Inn Christmas.

She loved taking pencil to paper, so she'd sketched her vision of the lobby, and then she'd drawn another for the new ballroom. The refresh projects kept her connected to her artistic skills.

She couldn't wait to show her sketches to Josie. Once they were approved, she could get to work placing the appropriate orders. This was going to be her biggest project to date and her most public one. The whole town would be judging her skills by this one project. Her stomach shivered with nerves.

With her sketch pad in a messenger bag and a to-go-cup of hot coffee in her hand, she made her way to the inn. She forced a smile to her lips. If she didn't look confident in her work, no one else would feel confident in it.

And yet as she entered the lobby, she immediately glanced at the front desk. Harvey wasn't there. She told herself it was a good thing he wasn't around. After all, he was the one who had broken her heart. Why would she want to see him?

She had her new career to focus on, and she enjoyed it. It gave her a new sense of purpose—a reason to get out of bed in the morning. It was a career she'd never even considered before. And she was so happy that this opportunity had come her way. And she wouldn't let Harvey's periodic presence at the inn ruin it for her. This island might be small, but it was big enough for the two of them.

As she approached the desk, Sara said, "Good morning."

"Hi. Is Josie in yet?"

Sara smiled and nodded. "Are you ready for your presentation?"

With Sara being married to her nephew Kent, she wasn't surprised that she knew about this important meeting. "I am." She patted her messenger bag. "I just hope she likes my sketches."

"I've seen your work, and you're very good. I'm sure she'll love it. Josie is back in the office. Would you like me to walk you back?"

Carol shook her head. "That won't be necessary. I know the way."

"Good luck."

"Thanks."

Behind her, the jingle of the door opening sounded. She moved past the desk toward the hallway leading to the administrative offices. Josie's office was at the end. Carol rapped her knuckles against the partially closed doorway.

"Come in."

Carol pushed the door fully open and entered. "Good morning." She noticed all of the work sitting on her niece's desk. "I hope you still have time for me."

Josie signed a paper, closed the file, and pushed it off to the side. "I definitely have time for you." She picked up a book from the other side of her desk. "By the way, have you read this book yet?"

Carol blinked and focused on the colorful, illustrated book cover. It was a cozy mystery. Her favorite genre to read. "I haven't. I believe that book just came out."

"Oh. Really?" Josie turned the book to look at the cover. "A guest left it behind in their room. When we contacted them, they said to give it to someone who would enjoy it. And since I don't read mysteries, I thought of you."

Carol knew the author, and she had been looking forward to reading it. "Are you sure?"

Josie nodded her head. "Go ahead and take it."

"Okay. You don't have to tell me twice." Carol took the book and placed it into her bag. She already had a book to finish reading and then she would start this one. "Thanks."

"Glad you'll enjoy it." Josie smiled. "What do you have for me?"

Carol took a seat, reached into her messenger bag, and retrieved her sketch pad. Before she showed her visions of the holiday décor to Josie, she explained that they were just drafts, and she could still make changes to them.

Josie waved for her to hand them over. Carol's stomach knotted up. *What if she hated them?*

When she placed the sketches in front of Josie, she was quiet as Josie studied them. Carol couldn't tell what she was thinking. Carol laced her fingers together to keep from fidgeting. She wanted to say something, but no words come to mind.

And then Josie smiled at her. She gushed over the plans. Then they went over each room in detail. Josie had a little bit of input to each of them. None of the changes were major. While Josie spoke, Carol took notes.

Once they'd gone over everything, Carol pulled out her laptop. She came prepared with online orders ready to place with priority shipping. It only took a few replacements until the orders were finalized. By the time the meeting was over, everything was ordered and would be delivered in the next couple of days.

"Aunt Carol, I'd like you to get started with the Christmas tree right away." Josie walked with her back toward the lobby.

"Do you have an artificial tree in storage?"

"Um, yes, but we aren't going to use it this year."

Carol was confused. "Do you want me to order a new one?" She worried that an artificial Christmas tree might be harder to get with Christmas in less than two weeks' time. In fact, this whole situation was of particularly short notice.

"No. I want a live tree."

"Live?" She hadn't anticipated that.

"Yes, a fresh cut one from the Christmas tree farm."

Carol struggled not to gape when she realized her niece was serious. She glanced down at her red reindeer sweater and black slacks. Not exactly the clothes she would have picked to go tramping around in the snow, searching for a Christmas tree. At least she had black snow boots on.

"What size tree do you have in mind? A six-footer?"

Josie shook her head. "This will be for in the reception room. It has twelve-foot ceilings. So I'm thinking a ten-foot tree."

Carol stopped walking and turned to her niece. "I... I don't think I can handle a tree that big on my own."

Josie nodded. "You're right." She glanced around the lobby. "Harvey, thanks for coming in early. Can you do me a favor and cut down a tree for the lobby?"

He nodded. "I'd be happy to do that."

Josie stepped to the side. "And my aunt will go with you to help select the right one."

Without giving either of them a chance to object to working together, Josie turned and headed back to her office. The sound of the office door closing echoed down the hallway.

Carol looked at Harvey, who didn't look any happier about this arrangement than she did. The last thing she wanted to do was spend the morning with the man who had dumped her. It had been a very long time since someone had done such a thing, and it didn't hurt any less regardless of her age.

And yet she couldn't manage such a large tree on her own. She inwardly groaned.

"Well, are you coming?" He frowned at her, like this had been her idea.

"Listen, I'm not any happier about this arrangement than you, but you don't have to be so grinchy."

His brows rose high on his forehead. "Grinchy? No one has ever called me that."

"Well. I have now." She knew what people normally called him: Santa. But there was nothing about him at the moment that was Santa-like.

He frowned at her. "I am not...um, grinchy."

She straightened her shoulders and tilted her chin upward ever so slightly. "Then prove it."

"What's that supposed to mean?"

"It means find your Christmas spirit. It's not like this is going to be a date or anything. It's work. Nothing more. There's no reason you have to be so grouchy about it."

The frown slipped from his face long enough for her to be reminded of how handsome he was. Her heart pitter-pattered just like it had done when they'd dated in the past. She refused to let herself fall for him again.

"Fine." He gave her a quick once-over. "Is that what you're planning to wear? You know that it just snowed last night."

She glanced down at her outfit. "I actually think this sweater is really cute. But I had no idea I was going out to cut down a tree when I picked out my clothes this morning."

"I need to attach a trailer to the back of the cart to haul the tree, and then I suppose we could stop by your place so you can change clothes."

She wasn't going to argue with him. "Then let's go."

This would be awkward, but they would get through it. After all, how long would it take to pick out a Christmas tree?

CHAPTER FIVE

THE SNOW CONTINUED TO fall.

And the wind kicked up the fallen snow and blew it around.

Harvey wanted to get this task over with quickly, but Carol was being picky about finding the perfect tree. Did one even exist? He didn't think so.

And there was the matter of his feet growing cold. Then Carol looked at him and smiled. A warmth swirled in his chest and pulsed out to his extremities. Maybe he wasn't so cold after all.

The Christmas tree farm was bustling with people. Young and old alike. Kids were laughing and running around. The adults were smiling as they set off on their own search for a "perfect" tree.

They had finished searching through the pre-cut trees, but none would do. Harvey's gaze moved to the sloping hillside that resembled a small forest of pine trees. He felt as though finding a tree Carol would approve of would be like searching for a needle in a pile of pine needles.

He held one of the hand saws offered by the farm. "Are you ready to begin up the hill?"

Carol gave the hillside a quick glance. "Yes. Let's do it. Remember we're searching for a blue spruce."

"Those are at the top of the hill," a worker at the farm called out.

Oh, lucky him. Harvey subdued a frustrated groan. It would mean carrying the tree that much farther.

As they started up the hill, Carol glanced over at him. "Are you okay?"

"You mean can I walk up this hill?" He didn't wait for her response. "If you're implying that I'm out of shape..."

"That's not what I meant." The pink in her cheeks from the cold air intensified to a rosy hue.

"I'll have you know that I walk five miles a day." Between the doctors and his daughter, they had him on a health regimen that included both diet and exercise. He was stronger now than he'd been in years.

"Really? That's impressive." The honesty of her words showed in her eyes. "I guess I should do something like that too."

His irritation slipped away. It'd been too long since they'd had a friendly conversation. And he missed how easy it used to be to talk to her.

"I didn't start out at five miles," Harvey said. "I worked up to it over the past year and a half." It was only then he realized just how long it'd been since his heart attack and subsequent bypass surgery. For the longest time, he never thought he would live this long. "I also have some weightlifting that I do every day."

"No wonder Josie asked you to help me with this. You're turning into a real-life Paul Bunyan."

Harvey let out a laugh—a genuine laugh—and it felt good. "I think you just insulted Mr. Bunyan."

"I don't know. Just wait until you start swinging that ax."

He held up the saw. "Hate to disappoint you, but all I have is this."

She pursed her lips. "Hm... It's not quite the same image with a saw."

A little smile pulled at the corners of his lips as he shook his head. He forgot how their conversation could go off on the strangest tangents. When he was with Carol, he'd learned to expect the unexpected. Some things hadn't changed.

He glanced around at all of the pine trees. To him, any of them would be fine. But every time he pointed one out to her, she rejected it for one reason or another.

And yet he kept looking for the right tree. Anything to end this outing as soon as possible. Because the more time he spent with Carol, the harder it was to remember why they couldn't pick up things where they'd left off.

It had started to snow at a pretty good clip, and he didn't want to end up getting his cart stuck in the snow. Even though it was possible to walk home, he wasn't thrilled about the prospect of such a cold hike.

His gaze settled on a tall evergreen. It was quite large. In fact, it might be too tall for the room, but it could be cut down to size.

"What about this one?" he asked.

Carol backtracked to him. She turned to the tree. "This one?"

He nodded. "It's perfect."

She tilted her head to the side as she visually inspected the tree. "You don't think it's too big for the room?"

He shrugged. "It can be trimmed."

"I don't know."

He let out a frustrated sigh. "I think you've looked at every tree on the hill."

"It has to be the right tree."

"And if you don't pick a tree soon, Christmas will be over, and it'll be the New Year."

She gaped at him. "I can't believe you said that. You know how important this is. The whole town will be at the inn this Christmas. Josie is counting on us to get this right."

"I don't think the whole town will be there. The ballroom isn't big enough to hold everyone at once."

She sighed. "You know what I mean."

"I don't know what you're worrying about. I've seen the work you've done at my daughter's bookshop and the Watsons' place. You did a wonderful job." It was the truth. Carol was quite talented. She came up with ideas for decorating he never would have thought of.

Carol shook her head. "This is different."

"You worry too much." He just wanted her to make a decision so they could get out of the cold.

"And you're too grinchy these days to be able to play Santa on Christmas Eve. You need to lighten up and enjoy the holidays." She didn't wait for him to respond before she walked away.

"I am not grinchy," he mumbled under his breath.

He was just guarded around Carol. He didn't want to let her get too close. His fingers moved to his chest. With his winter coat on, he couldn't feel the vertical scar on his chest. They said with time it would fade, but in his mind it would never diminish.

Swoosh.

Thud.

Bits of snow cascaded over his shoulder and head. The cold bits fell and landed inside the collar of his shirt. *Brr...* The snow melted and dripped down his back.

He swung around to see where the snowball had come from.

Swish.

Thud.

Another snowball struck him straight in the chest. *Really?* His gaze landed on Carol, who leaned over, scooping up snow and pressing it into a ball.

When she straightened, she had a big grin that lit up her whole face and made her blue eyes twinkle. *Gorgeous. Simply gorgeous.*

And then she raised her arm. She pulled her hand back before she sent the snowball flying. He ducked, letting the snowball collide with the pine tree behind him.

He hadn't been involved in a snowball fight since his daughter was a kid. But he wasn't too old to fire off a few.

"You're in trouble now." He bent over, stretching his arms out at both sides. As he drew them together, snow gathered in his palms.

He straightened. His hands mushed the snow into a ball. He scanned the landscape, seeking out his target. Carol was bent over, gathering more snow for ammunition. He pulled back and let the snowball fly.

It hit its mark. *Yes!*

Carol let out a squeal as she jerked upright and dusted off her backside. "That was a low blow."

"Really? I thought it hit the bull's eyes." He sent her a teasing smile.

She glared at him, but he caught the hint of a smile pulling at the corners of her lips. He let himself live in the moment.

They sent snowballs flying. Both of them ducking just in time.

This wasn't what a grinchy person would do. This was too much fun. And it was thanks to Carol. He'd forgotten what it was like not to worry about his health and just let himself live in the moment. The laughter and fun had to be good medicine for his heart.

But as the snow came down faster, the fun ended. It was time to get back to reality. He couldn't forget the reason they were no longer together. Nothing had changed, but despite his constant internal warnings, he kept having to fight the smile that tugged at the corners of his lips.

———*ell*———

The tree was perfect.

Later that afternoon, the open boxes of decorations were arranged on tables near the Christmas tree in the lobby of the Brass Anchor Inn. Carol was excited to trim the tree. It was one of her favorite holiday traditions. She just hoped it lived up to Josie's expectations.

It didn't help that she was utterly distracted by thoughts of Harvey. After she'd figuratively waved the white flag to end the snowball fight, she found her cheeks hurt from smiling so much. It had been a long time since that had happened to her.

Afterward, she noticed Harvey wasn't frowning as much. In fact, she'd caught him smiling a time or two. He might have smiled more if the temperatures hadn't dropped and the winds hadn't picked up. It really put a damper on their fun, making them focus on getting the tree back to the cart as quickly as possible.

Once they got back to the inn, it was quickly decided that this tree was too wide for the lobby.

They moved it to the ballroom. Harvey helped her anchor the tree in a stand that was attached to a large wood base.

"What are you still doing here?" Josie came to stand next to her.

Carol turned to her. "I, uh...just thought you might want some help this evening."

Josie glanced around at the various boxes. "I think we're good. Thank you for all you did. But take the evening off. There will be lots to do tomorrow when the first shipment of decorations arrives."

Carol knew her niece was right. There would be a lot to do tomorrow. The tree would look amazing when she was done with it.

"I'll see you at your parents' place for dinner, won't I?" Carol asked.

"I wouldn't miss it. See you there."

Carol went home but didn't have time to do much before it was time to leave for dinner. She loved being included in her sister's big dinners. They were so warm and filled with lively conversation.

She drove over and was excited to find a parking spot in front of the house. Someone must have just left. She zipped right into the spot with a triumphant smile.

As she walked to the porch, she could hear the murmur of conversation emanating from inside the house. The hum of voices broadened her smile. There was nothing better than a family get-together.

Carol's mother had raised her to never show up empty-handed. She arrived with two pies: one cherry and the other apple. With her sister's rapidly expanding family, she hoped two pies would be enough.

Lucky for her, the door opened. And there stood Josie. "Let me take those for you."

"Thank you."

As Carol shrugged off her coat and took off her snow boots, she inhaled the delicious aroma of tomatoes, sausage, and oregano. Since she forgot to eat lunch that day, her stomach rumbled its approval. Her sister loved being surrounded by her family as much as she loved cooking for them. This was going to be a great evening full of the most delicious food and good conversation. It would give her a chance to think about something besides Harvey and how his presence filled her with conflicting emotions.

Carol followed the aroma to the spacious kitchen, where she found her sister Patty with her hands in the sink. Carol washed up and then grabbed a drying towel. "You know, if your family keeps growing, you're going to have to get a bigger kitchen."

"It isn't always like this." Patty glanced over her shoulder and smiled as her family was crowded around the island. "But I love having them here."

George, Patty's husband, stepped into the kitchen. He walked up to his wife and kissed her cheek. "The table is set, and I put the folding table in the living room. How much longer until the food is ready?"

Patty glanced at the timer on the stove. "Four minutes until the lasagna is done."

"Okay. Do you need anything else?" When Patty told him no, he said, "I'm going to watch some of the game while I wait. Yell, if you need anything."

Carol couldn't help but daydream what it might have been like if she and her husband had had kids. They'd tried, but it never worked out. And eventually they found themselves happy with the life they'd created.

Just then Owen bumped into her. "Sorry, Aunt Carol."

"No problem." Then again, she wasn't all alone. She was a part of this family, and they were wonderful.

CHAPTER SIX

T HIS WASN'T SUCH A good idea after all.

Harvey drove to the Turners' house with a poinsettia and a box of cookies from The Elegant Bakery on the seat next to him. In the past, he'd always had the perfect excuse not to attend these Turner family dinners—he had been getting some sleep before working the night shift at the inn. But now that he worked the day shift, he couldn't come up with a legitimate excuse not to attend. And this time the invitation hadn't come from his daughter, but rather her mother-in-law, Patty, who had insisted he must attend. Patty had stressed the fact that now that their children were married, they were family. He couldn't find an argument to that statement.

He'd wanted to ask if Carol had been invited to dinner, but he didn't want Patty to read anything into the question. Since Carol and Patty were sisters, he imagined Carol would be there. He knew this was the first of many run-ins. But there was no reason they both had to be miserable. After dinner, he would just thank his hosts and quietly slip away.

He slowed down as he neared the Turners' house. A solid line of golf carts were parked on both sides of the street. He supposed this was what happened when your family expanded.

On the next block, he found a parking spot. He grabbed the poinsettia and cookies before heading down the sidewalk. He stepped up to the front door and knocked. The door was immediately opened by Josie, who smiled at him.

As he stepped inside, he was met with the aroma of tomato sauce. His mouth watered. Maybe agreeing to this dinner wasn't such a bad idea after all.

The large kitchen was at the back of the house. And it was filled with wall-to-wall people. Carol stood next to the sink, drying a frying pan. She was quick to notice him. A hesitant smile lifted the corners of her lips ever so slightly.

Patty turned to him. "Harvey, I'm so glad you made it." When he held out the poinsettia and cookies to her, she smiled. After drying her hands, she took them. "You really shouldn't have." She looked at the flowers. "Thank you."

"Merry Christmas."

His gaze moved to Carol, who had just straightened after putting the skillet in a lower cabinet. Might as well get over the awkward part. "Hello, Carol."

"Hi, Harvey."

Cutting down a pine tree was one thing, but having a cozy family dinner together was quite another. On second thought, he should make his apologies and leave early. There was no point in making this evening uncomfortable for both of them.

He opened his mouth but before he could utter a word, Melinda stepped into the kitchen. "Hey, Dad. Glad you could make it. Liam and Tate are watching the game in the living room." She gestured for him to follow.

Harvey didn't want to make a scene, so he quietly followed her. Actually, this might be a better way to make his escape. He'd say hello to his son-in-law and Tate, then he'd be on his way.

George Turner was sitting in the living room. "Hey, Harvey. Have a seat. I have the game on. It's a tie game."

As George continued to talk, it didn't look like Harvey would be making an exit any time soon. Not that it would be a hardship. The house was big enough to avoid Carol. Besides, he enjoyed his time with his daughter's in-laws. As he chatted with George and Liam, he let himself relax.

The lively conversation centered around football and the playoffs. It carried on until they were called to sit down for dinner. George talked to him the whole way to the dining room table. Melinda gestured for him to sit next to her. He eyed up Patty's lasagna and salivated.

Harvey settled into his seat at the exact moment that someone sat down across from him. He looked up, and his gaze connected with familiar blue eyes. His heart thumped. It was Carol. And she was looking directly at him.

This could be awkward. Maybe he should switch seats. *Yes.* That sounded like a good idea. He glanced around, finding all of the seats were taken. Then again, it wasn't like he could just quietly change seats without everyone noticing. He was trapped.

"Harvey?" Carol said.

He hesitated to meet her gaze. If he didn't know better, he'd think his daughter had set them up, but there was no way she would do something like that at her in-laws.

When he lifted his gaze and met hers, Carol whispered, "It's okay. It's just dinner."

Melinda glanced over at Carol and then him. "Is something wrong?"

They both shook their heads.

Melinda narrowed her gaze on them. "Are you sure?"

They both nodded.

When Melinda turned to speak to her husband, Harvey glanced back at Carol. She frowned at him before glancing away. It would appear she wasn't any happier with this cozy dinner than he was. When Patty sat next to her, they talked, and it was as though she was to forget about his presence. It should have made him feel better, but it didn't.

Thankfully, Owen Turner sat down next to him. He always struck Harvey as the quiet type. Still, it wouldn't hurt to make a little conversation.

"It was really nice of your mother to include me," Harvey said.

"She loves to have a house full of people." Owen handed over his plate for lasagna.

"That's right." Patty placed a square of lasagna on the plate.

Next it was Harvey's turn to hand over his plate. "What have you been up to lately?"

Owen's eyes widened, as though he were surprised Harvey was trying to make conversation with him. "I...uh, I've been working in the garage."

Garage? Interesting, considering automobiles weren't allowed on the island. "Are you working on your golf cart?"

Owen shook his head, then took a bite of pasta. After he swallowed, he said, "I was working on the MG."

Had he heard him correctly? Harvey hesitated, replaying what he'd heard. "You have a car?"

Owen nodded. "It's not actually my car. It was my great-grandfather's. It's a 1939 MG. I like to work with my hands, and with the first vintage grand prix this summer, I plan to enter it."

"Grand prix, here?" How had he missed this? Had he been that distracted by Carol's presence at the inn that he'd missed this news?

Owen nodded. "They just announced it yesterday. It's going to be this summer. It'll be a part of the celebration for the grand opening of the hospital."

"That sounds exciting."

"Of course, they're going to be inviting people from all over the country. Still, there are a few of us that have antique cars in our garages from the old days before they restricted automobiles on the island."

He nodded in understanding. "How's the car?"

"Not in good shape." Owen went on to tell him about all of the things he needed to work on to make it road-worthy.

Harvey enjoyed the distraction. Although, he did find himself glancing periodically across the table. There were a couple times when his gaze met Carol's, but then they would both turn away.

He resumed his conversation with Owen. Quite honestly, he didn't know a lot about cars, but he was drawn in by Owen's enthusiasm. Harvey would have offered a helping hand, but he thought he'd be more of a hindrance than a help.

When dinner concluded, Harvey was more than ready to make his exit. Because having Carol so close and yet so far away was pure torture. There were a number of times he'd thought of something he'd wanted to say to her, but he hesitated. He didn't know if he should say anything further to her.

With everyone moving toward the living room, he felt this was his chance to make a quick exit. He started in that direction. He spotted his coat hanging near the door.

He'd made it to the foyer when he heard, "Hey, Dad. Wait."

He inwardly groaned. He loved his daughter dearly, but sometimes she had terrible timing. And he didn't want to explain to her why he was trying to make a quick escape.

When he paused and turned, Melinda was standing there. She gave him a hug. "Thanks for coming."

"No problem. It was nice of them to include me."

"Be careful on the way home," she said.

"I will. You be careful too. With the temps dropping, it's going to be icy out there."

After Melinda walked away, Harvey grabbed his coat and slipped it on. He was almost out the door. Just a few more steps.

"You aren't leaving early because of me, are you?"

Carol. He once more inwardly groaned. He forced a smile to his face and turned. "No. Of course not."

"It's okay. I won't keep you. I just wanted to say that it appears we'll both be at these dinners every now and then, so if there's anything I can do to make them less awkward, just let me know."

He nodded. "And feel free to let me know if there's anything I can do."

She nodded. "I will. I noticed you and Owen had a lot to talk about."

He gave her a brief summary about Owen's car.

Her brow arched in disbelief. "You're interested in car repairs?"

"Yes." She knew him well enough to know he didn't know the radiator from the battery. Still, he wasn't going to admit he'd used the conversation as a distraction from her.

She frowned as though she knew he was lying. "Is it possible we can be friends again?"

Her request wasn't unreasonable. He nodded. "Of course. We've never not been friends."

A smile lifted her lips, and this time her eyes shone with happiness. Her beautiful face practically glowed, causing his heart to pound. He told himself to look away, but he couldn't take his gaze off her.

"Good." Even her voice had a happy tone. "I wouldn't want to lose our friendship. I'll see you tomorrow at the inn."

"Good night." He turned and opened the door. Without any further interruptions, he made it outside.

On the ride home, he replayed the conversation with Carol. Maybe he shouldn't have agreed to their friendship, but how could he turn her down? And when she smiled, his heart had hammered in his chest. He was in trouble. Big trouble.

CHAPTER SEVEN

Ten days before Christmas

IT HAD BEEN A busy day.

Carol smothered a yawn. She'd worked diligently all day completing the final details on the lobby. It looked festive enough that they could hold the town's festivities in there.

She reached for her insulated cup with some coffee in it. She needed the boost because her evening wasn't over when she went home. In fact, she couldn't go straight home. She needed to stop at the market to pick up some groceries. Tonight, she was baking Christmas cookies. Perhaps she would play a Christmas movie in the background. She liked that idea.

This was the big moment—the final inspection. These events always made Carol a bit nervous. Even though she liked the final product, it didn't mean her client would feel the same way.

There was an artificial pencil tree in the one corner with white and silver ball ornaments. The twinkle lights were multi-colored. But the highlight of the display was a Christmas village.

In the end, the display cases with Bluestar's history had been moved to make room for the display tables with the village and an antique train that Josie had uncovered in the attic right here at the inn.

Carol was surprised the train still worked. She didn't know exactly how old the train was, but it definitely had been around for a long time.

The miniature houses and shops were also antiques. She'd added lights to all of the structures. It gave them a warm glow. Carol had so much fun putting it all together with little Christmas trees and antique cars. She used polyester fiberfill stuffing for the snow that covered the ground.

She'd had the forethought to create *DO NOT TOUCH* signs to place around the display. She knew children and the young at heart would instinctively reach out to touch the display. Everything about the display was fragile.

Carol double-checked that everything was connected and then crossed her fingers that it would all work. She hadn't expected so many wires would be needed to light up everything in the village.

She was just about to plug the wires into the outlet when she heard, "Oh, wow! It's done."

Carol straightened and turned to her niece, who was smiling brightly. "Yes, it is."

"I love it. Does it work?"

"I was just about to plug it in."

"This is great." Josie silently clapped her hands together as she smiled brightly.

Carol moved between the Christmas tree and the display table. She knelt down and plugged in the power strip. Immediately, she heard the train clicking down the tracks.

She straightened and hoped when she turned that everything would be lit up. She turned and scanned the display. Everything appeared to be working properly. She expelled a pent-up breath.

Her gaze moved to the red skirt that she'd placed on the table. She'd taped a long strand of colored twinkle lights around the perimeter of the table.

Her gaze followed the antique train through a tunnel, down the tracks, and then over a bridge. So far, so good. And then her gaze skimmed over the small-town setting in the middle.

She glanced over at Josie, who was still taking in the scene. "I hope this was what you'd imagined."

Josie shook her head, and Carol's heart plummeted. She'd tried so hard to make it spectacular. She knew how much both of their professional reputations were riding on this holiday display and the one she would create in the ballroom.

"Just tell me what's wrong, and I'll fix it." Carol's gaze moved to the display, trying to figure out how she could make it better.

"Aunt Carol, this isn't what I imagined. It's so much better." Josie's eyes shimmered with happy tears.

Her niece leaned over and gave her a hug. "Thank you for all you did. The guests and town are absolutely going to love it."

When Josie pulled back, Carol said, "I'm so happy you like it. Are you sure there's nothing that needs to be changed?"

"Absolutely nothing. It's perfect just the way it is. I can't wait to show Lane when he gets back from California."

"Will he be home soon?"

"I hope." The smile slipped from her face.

"It's some sort of business emergency. He promised to be back as soon as possible."

"At least you have a lot to keep you busy while he's gone." The first Christmas event would be held the day after tomorrow. This place would be hopping with visitors.

"I know, but I miss him so much."

"And I'm certain he's missing you too."

"I wish I could figure out what to get him for Christmas. I have a couple of things, but I want something special."

Carol patted her arm. "Stop worrying so much. He already has the most special gift of all—your love."

"Aw...Aunt Carol, I never knew you were such a romantic."

Her thoughts immediately turned to Harvey. She gave a quick glance over her shoulder to see if he'd overheard their conversation. She blew out a relieved breath when she noticed he wasn't standing at the reception desk.

She turned back to Josie. She sent her a smile and a nonchalant shrug. "A woman has to have her secrets." Anxious to change the subject, she said, "I was thinking about heading to the ballroom and work on those decorations."

"Do you need help?"

She glanced at the clock on the wall. "Actually, with it getting so late, I think I'll just get an early start in the morning."

She'd already made up a schedule in order to get things done on time. And as of that moment, she was right on target. Pushing too hard would only lead to mistakes and she didn't want that to happen.

It was a lot of work for one person, and the timeline was shorter than she would like, but she would meet it. This was her chance to prove to the locals that they needed to hire her to redecorate their businesses and homes.

Speaking of which, she moved to her bag and withdrew a couple of signs. One she placed under the Christmas tree. The other she situated at the end of the table. It read: *Refresh by Turner Furnishings*. In smaller letters it read: *Carol Carmichael, decorator*. Her shoulders straightened, and a smile pulled at the corner of her lips as she stared at the signs.

Buzz.

"That's my phone." Josie pulled it from her pocket. She glanced at the screen and sighed. "It's work." She looked up. "Thank you again. You do amazing work."

And then Josie pressed the phone to her ear and walked away.

Carol cleaned up her things. She stashed the empty boxes in the storage room so they would be available when the holidays were over and it was time to take down the decorations.

She made her way to the spare office where she was keeping her things. She slipped on her coat and wrapped a white scarf around her neck. After pulling on her gloves, she headed for the door.

The wind was still blowing. The cold seeped through every gap in her coat and chilled her to the bone. She opened the door on her cart and got inside. She put her key in the ignition and turned. Nothing happened.

She tried again. And again. And again.

It was dead. *Ugh!*

~ elle ~

Her plan was starting to work.

Josie had witnessed the smile on her aunt's face when she'd finished speaking with Harvey the night before at dinner. Josie didn't know what had been said, but it must have been something good.

She also noticed the frown lines on Harvey's face had lessened. They were good for each other. If only they could figure that out for themselves.

And that was why she might have done a little something else to help push them together. She was in the hallway just outside of the ballroom when her phone rang again. When she checked the caller ID and saw it was Lane, her heart skipped a beat.

She pressed the phone to her ear. "Are you coming home?"

He let out a laugh. "Well, hello to you too."

"Sorry. Hello. Are you coming home soon?"

He laughed again. "I promise I'll be home as soon as I can."

She sighed. "But it's not going to be today, is it?"

"I'm afraid not. Are you missing me?"

"No." Her answer was too quick.

"For some reason I don't believe you. What have you been up to?"

The way he said it was like he knew she was up to something he probably wouldn't approve of. "Why do I have to be up to anything?"

"So, you are up to something. What is it?"

"If you want to know, you'll have to come home and find out for yourself."

"Now I'm really worried."

She let out a laugh. "Maybe you shouldn't go away."

"I'll keep that in mind for the future," Lane said. "Now, what has you so distracted?"

"I'm not distracted."

"Oh, yes you are. You haven't even asked me what I got you for Christmas."

"Maybe I already found it."

"I know you didn't because I didn't hide it in the house. I knew you'd look for it. Now, tell me what you're up to." There was a firm tone to his voice.

She sighed. "If you must know, my aunt's cart is dead, and I'm hoping Harvey will help her out and give her a ride home."

"And how would you know her cart is dead?"

She sighed again. "Has anyone ever told you that you are very curious?"

"Just answer the question."

Heat swirled in her chest and rushed up to her cheeks. She loved Lane, but sometimes she didn't like how well he knew her. "Fine. I might have turned on her lights earlier and left them on."

"Josie..."

"Well, if you didn't want to know, you shouldn't have asked."

She pictured him shaking his head. "You shouldn't meddle."

She shrugged. "They just need a little push in the right direction."

"Josie, this is going to blow up in your face. And then I'm going to say I told you so."

"And what are you going to say if they find their happily ever after?"

"That you got very lucky."

She would show him. She knew Harvey and Aunt Carol belonged together. But this matchmaking appeared as though it would take a little more effort than she'd initially expected.

And then she spotted Harvey walking in her direction. She needed to speak to him before the opportunity slipped by them. "I have to go."

"Josie, don't do this."

"Gotta go. I love you."

"I love you too."

No sooner had she pressed the end button than she said, "Harvey?"

He came to a stop next to her and peered in the doorway of the ballroom. "What do you think of the tree?"

"I think you two make a good team." She smiled at him. "It's the perfect tree. When it's decorated, it will look spectacular."

Harvey nodded. "It took a bit to find it. But I think you're right. It fits well in the room."

Now it was time to put the next step of her plan in motion. "Harvey, would you mind going outside and checking the sidewalks? With all of the wind, I worry the snow will drift. You might need to get Justin to clear them again."

He nodded. "I'm on my way home. I'll check them before I go."

"Thanks. And have a good evening."

There were ten more days until Christmas. It was enough time to make Project:...hm... Project: Mistletoe a success.

Speaking of which...mistletoe. She needed mistletoe. Lots of mistletoe. A smile pulled at the corner of her lips. It would come in handy for more than just Aunt Carol and Harvey.

Her thoughts turned to her handsome husband. Just as quickly she felt a pang of loneliness. He couldn't come home soon enough.

CHAPTER EIGHT

H E DIDN'T KNOW WHAT Josie was worried about.

The sidewalks looked fine.

Harvey stuffed his hands into his coat pockets as he made his way along the length of the large porch. Even though it was only a few minutes after four, it was already dark outside.

The parking lot lights illuminated the area. That was when he heard some sort of clicking sound. He didn't see anything. But then he heard the unusual sound again.

Then he noticed someone getting out of a cart. Was that Carol? He'd recalled her leaving a little while ago. What was she still doing in the parking lot? Maybe he should go investigate. *No.* It was none of his business.

And yet, he remained rooted to that spot. She moved around the cart. What was she doing?

Before he realized it, he had made his way down the steps. He'd come this far; he might as well go the rest of the way. When he neared her cart, she was removing things from the passenger seat.

When she glanced over at him, she jumped. Pressing a hand to her chest, she said, "You gave me a start."

He wasn't trying to sneak up on her. "Sorry. I was just checking to see if you needed some help."

"My cart won't start."

He wasn't surprised. The temperature was dropping. "Try again."

"It won't do any good." When he gave her an imploring look, she complied.

She turned the key, and as expected nothing happened. Nothing at all. It was probably her batteries. They most likely needed to be charged, and that would take time.

He intended to tell her to go back inside the inn to wait for a ride because it was too cold to walk, but when he opened his mouth, something quite different came out. "Come on. I'll give you a ride."

She shook her head. "I'm fine."

Really? She was going to choose one of the coldest evenings of the year to be stubborn. He choked down his frustration. He didn't want to be accused of sounding grinchy again.

"You're not fine," he stated firmly. "It's dark and cold with the temperatures continuing to drop. Let me help you."

She was quiet for a moment, as though giving his words due consideration. He didn't know what there was to think about, but at least she hadn't just outright refused his offer this time.

"I can walk." She once more grabbed her things from the passenger seat and got out.

Before he could argue the point, a strong gust of frigid wind rushed past them. It sent a shiver down his spine and had him wishing he'd put on gloves. He stuffed his hands into his coat pockets.

Carol hesitated. Would she be too stubborn to accept his help?

As the wind kicked up again, his patience wore thin. "Tonight isn't the night for walking."

"Fine. If you're sure it's not a problem."

"It's not." Even if it was, he wouldn't tell her.

He took the bags from her hand and headed for his cart, hoping she would fall in step behind him. He didn't slow down to glance back, because he didn't want to give her a chance to mount yet another argument. It was just too cold for that out there.

His cart was parked off to the side in the employee parking section. He placed her belongings in the backseat. When he turned, he was relieved to see she had decided to follow him. But he supposed she didn't have much of a choice, since he had her possessions.

He opened the door for her. Once she was seated, he closed it before rushing around the front of the vehicle to get inside. The older he got, the more he noticed the cold. It wasn't so long ago that below freezing weather didn't bother him, but lately it felt as though the cold leached into his bones and didn't want to leave.

He started the cart without a problem and turned on the heater. He adjusted it to its warmest setting with the blower on high and then backed out of the parking spot.

When his gaze caught sight of the worried look on Carol's face, he said, "Don't worry. I'll charge your batteries for you. That's probably all it needs. Tomorrow you should be good to go."

"Th-Thank you." As the wind kicked up, she wrapped her arms over her chest. She looked at him like she wanted to ask him a question but then glanced away, as though she'd thought better of it. "I hope so. I have so much to do. And walking everywhere will really slow me down."

He wondered why she was putting so much pressure on herself. When he first heard that she'd taken on the refresh job at the inn, he'd thought it was because she had too much time on her hands. Now he wondered if there was something else that was driving her.

Maybe things weren't going that well with her family. Although, that was hard to believe because the Turners were a great family—friendly, welcoming and kind. Still, sometimes there were things that went on in families that no one from the outside could see. He hoped it wasn't the case. He knew how much Carol loved her family, especially her sister.

"Work can wait," he said. "You should take the evening to rest and relax. You must be tired after that snowball fight, um...I mean the Christmas tree hunt."

She shook her head. "I don't have time to rest. I have some baking to do this evening. Oh no!"

His foot automatically let up on the accelerator as his gaze searched the roadway for a human or animal. "What's wrong?"

She shook her head again. "It's nothing for you to worry about."

It was too late for that. Not seeing anything in the roadway, he pressed on the accelerator once more. "Just tell me. Maybe I can help you."

"You've already helped me enough."

He resisted the urge to roll his eyes. Not sure what was going on with her, he pulled off to the side of the road and stopped. "What is it you need?"

She hesitated. "The market. I need some baking supplies, but I can walk."

"I thought we already had this conversation. This evening isn't a good time for a walk. We'll just make a detour." He pulled back onto the road.

"But you have to go back to work."

He lifted his arm to check his watch. "My shift ended four minutes ago. Now, I'm all yours." The words slipped past his lips before he realized how it would sound. "I... I mean I'm all yours to do a little bit of shopping." It didn't sound any better the second time around.

"Thank you. I'd appreciate the help. I honestly wasn't looking forward to carrying home the flour and sugar."

He was grateful she didn't say anything about his terrible choice in words. He didn't know what had gotten into him. He didn't make those sorts of mistakes very often. And this one was a doozy.

He stopped at the market. There weren't many people there. Probably no one wanted to go out in that brutal wind. He couldn't blame them.

When he grabbed a basket, Carol said, "Oh, no. We're going to need a cart."

He returned the basket and grabbed a cart. "How many baking supplies are you planning to buy?"

She reached into her purse and pulled out a shopping list. She held it out to him. "Just these."

He looked at the list, which was rather lengthy. "And you were going to carry all of that home?"

She turned the list around and glanced at it. "Well, I probably couldn't carry it all in one trip."

He let out a laugh. "You couldn't carry all of it in three trips." He loved how her cheeks took on a rosy hue. "Come on. I think it's going to take us a bit to find everything on that list."

He pushed the cart, and she put things in it. He hadn't gone grocery shopping with anyone since his wife had passed on. He'd forgotten how nice it was to share these sorts of mundane tasks.

She shouldn't have done it.

She shouldn't have let him go shopping with her.

Because now Carol felt indebted to Harvey. He'd been so kind and patient as she'd tried to decide between the milk chocolate or white chocolate chips, and then there was the debate between red or green sprinkles. She'd ended up buying them all because she just couldn't make up her mind. Her inability to make decisions might have something to do with the handsome man standing next to her, who was making her heart beat erratically.

After shopping, Harvey, being quite the gentleman, insisted on helping her carry the bags into her second-floor apartment. It was just a little one-bedroom apartment, but it was enough space for her, especially since she wasn't home that much.

Before she'd moved to Bluestar, she didn't think there would be that many things for locals to do. But in warmer weather, she found herself walking on the beach every morning and sometimes in the evening. She spent a lot of time at her sister's place, and she'd joined a Bridge club, but they took a break for the holidays.

And then there was her new job. When she had downtime, she found herself researching various home decorating styles, various forms of lighting, and so many other decorating details. She was constantly learning something, and she loved it. It had taken her years to find an occupation that she was passionate about, and now she was going to make the most of it.

Plus, she found it so rewarding when her clients' eyes lit up at the sight of the completed project; it was almost magical. And then to hear that she'd made their vision a reality, it didn't get better than that.

"Where would you like this?" Harvey's voice interrupted her thoughts.

She glanced over to find him holding some kitchen towels that were part of a special buy at the market. They were white with candy canes on one, another with snowmen, and the third one had an old-fashioned red pick-up truck with a green wreath on the front end. How was she supposed to pass them up?

"You can just put them on the bar stool. I'll launder them later." She moved to put the eggs in the fridge. When she turned back to the bags on the counter and pulled out a frozen pizza, she got an idea. "How would you feel about some pizza?"

His brows rose. "Uh... You don't have to do that."

"I know. But I can't eat this whole thing by myself." That wasn't exactly true. She loved leftover cold pizza for breakfast, but she felt obligated to somehow repay his kindness. When he hesitated, it dawned on her that it might not have been the ideal menu. "Oh, wait. You probably shouldn't eat pizza. Let me see what else I have to make." She opened the fridge.

"Don't worry. I'm fine."

She searched for the head of lettuce she'd picked up the other day. When she visually examined it, she sighed with relief. "I've got lettuce."

"Carol, thanks but I don't want a salad."

"You don't?" When he shook his head, she said, "I just thought you were eating healthy. But it's all right. If you don't want salad, I'm sure I can figure out something else." She opened the fridge again and peered inside.

"How about I share that pizza with you?"

She glanced over her shoulder at him. "Are you sure?"

He nodded. "I haven't had a pizza in a long time. It sounds good."

"But should you have it? What would your doctor say?" That question earned her a distinct frown.

"Don't start sounding like my daughter, or you'll be eating that pizza by yourself. After my bypass, Melinda became a mother hen. She's been fussing over me. You'd never know by the way she acts that I'm the parent and she is the child."

Carol held up her hands. "I plead innocence. No mother hen here. One pizza coming up."

While she preheated the oven, she noticed he was busy emptying the bags and placing the items on the counter for her. It would be so easy to imagine them doing this on a regular basis. As fast as the errant thought came to her, she dismissed it. She had no room in her life for a man.

She had to stay focused on her job. Without a nest egg to fall back on, she had to keep working. However, she recalled a particular conversation with her nephew Kent. He'd made it abundantly clear that her position was only temporary, unless there was a steady stream of business. And lately, business had been slow. The thought weighed on her.

She moved quickly, putting the supplies away. While the pizza baked, she pulled out her cookie recipes. If she was going to finish them that evening, she had to get started right away.

Harvey made himself comfortable at the counter. "What are the cookies for?"

"I plan to take them to the inn tomorrow." When his eyes lit up, she said, "Not for you."

He frowned. "Then who are they for?"

She shrugged. "Guests and visitors."

"I don't understand. The inn gets baked goods from The Elegant Bakery."

"This isn't to replace them. I talked with Josie, and she said it would be fine to put out my business cards along with the sign for the refresh business. Anyway, I got the idea that I'd put some Christmas cookies with them, and it might draw more people."

Harvey nodded. "It sounds like a great idea. But it's a lot of effort."

Carol shrugged. "But this gives me an excuse to bake."

"Something tells me there's more to the story than that."

"Perhaps." Wanting to change the subject, she said, "What kind of cookies do you like?"

He shrugged. "I don't know."

"You must have one that you like a little more than the others. Out with it. What's your favorite Christmas cookie?" When he didn't say anything, she offered a suggestion. "How about sugar cookies?"

He shrugged once more. "They're okay."

"But..."

"They're kind of boring."

"Boring?" She loved them, but when he nodded, she knew there were a lot of other cookies she could make.

She opened her cabinet and surveyed the contents. Luckily, she'd bought extra supplies at the store. And then she got an idea.

She turned back to him. "Do you like chai?"

He nodded.

"Good. I'm going to make sugar cookies and chai cookies."

She returned the recipes to the kitchen drawer. She searched through her grandmother's recipes until she found one for sugar cookies and another for chai cookies. She placed both recipe cards on the counter. Since she was in a hurry, she warmed the butter in the microwave at half power. She did the same for the cream cheese. By the time the pizza was out of the oven, she had two batches of dough for the cookies mixed and chilling in the fridge.

Harvey sliced the pizza while she poured them some lemon-lime soda. And then they sat side by side at the counter. Harvey surprised her by making small talk. It wasn't about anything important, but it was what friends would do.

And maybe it wouldn't be so bad to be friends again. But that was all it would be. She wasn't going to trust him with her heart again.

He should leave.

And yet he didn't move.

Harvey enjoyed watching Carol move about the kitchen with such familiarity. And when she swiped at a strand of hair in her face and in the process got a dab of cookie dough on her cheek, he longed to reach out and wipe it away for her. It took all of his self-control to keep his arm at his side.

He could no longer deny that he'd missed Carol's company in the past year since his heart attack—since he'd had to face his own mortality. He hadn't pushed Carol out of his life because of anything she'd done. Far from it. She was an amazingly kind woman.

He'd pushed her away to spare her. He knew what it was to grieve for a loved one. And Carol had already been through her own loss. He couldn't put her through that again.

He'd attempted to push Melinda away, but he'd failed miserably. His daughter was stubborn just like her mother had been. When he pushed, Melinda pushed back harder until he gave up the fight.

When it came to his surgery, the odds had been against him. He didn't think he was going to make it through the daunting procedure. But then he'd miraculously survived the triple bypass.

Although he couldn't shake the feeling that time was running out on him.

He'd told himself that it wouldn't be fair to keep Carol in his life and have her watch him decline. She'd already been through so much with her husband. He cared too much about her to put her through another health crisis. There was no hiding from how close he'd come to dying, because there was a scar on his chest as well as his daily meds, his diet restrictions, and his new exercise routine.

And yet now as he sat in Carol's warm kitchen, he couldn't think of any other place he'd rather be. For the moment, he felt like the man he used to be—instead of the broken man, who felt like his better years were behind him.

Perhaps that was why he'd indulged in a slice of mushroom pizza.

"Would you like some more?" Carol asked.

He eyed the pizza. *Maybe another slice wouldn't hurt.* He handed her his plate.

When she reached for it, their fingers touched. It was like static electricity arced between them. The sensation pulsed up his arm and settled in his chest. His heart thump-thumped like that of a twenty-year-old.

His gaze rose to meet hers. How was it that when she was around, he felt years younger?

She was so beautiful. He thought of telling her that, but at the last moment, he bit back the words. That would be taking this moment too far.

Carol pulled the plate away from him, breaking their contact. It was as though he'd been awakened from some sort of spell. Noticing that his mouth was dry, he reached for his glass and took a long drink of the icy cold soda.

Carol glanced at the wall clock. "You'll want to be going soon so you don't miss Twinkle Light Night."

He nodded. "You're coming, aren't you?"

She shook her head. "I don't think so."

"Why not?"

"Uh... You know, with my cart being broken down and all."

"Oh, that's right." How could he have forgotten that? When they were in close proximity to each other, his mind seemed to wonder. "I can give you a ride."

She shook her head. "You've already done enough to help me. I can't impose on you again."

"Nonsense. I'm going to the tree lighting. It would be nothing to take you and then drop you off here afterward."

"But I have the cookies to bake." She moved to the fridge and removed a bowl of chilled dough.

"I'll help you." He got up and washed his hands. "You just have to tell me what to do."

"We'll do the easy ones first," she said.

He sent her a puzzled look. "Which one is the easy one?"

She smiled at him. "The chai cookies. All you have to do is roll one-inch balls." She grabbed a little bit of dough, rolled it between her palms. "Like this." She held it up for him to see. "Then you place them on the tray and press your thumb in the middle. Like this. Think you can manage that?"

"Perhaps."

"And while you work on those, I'll start rolling out the sugar cookies."

"I haven't done something like this since I was a kid."

"Seriously? Your wife didn't bake?"

He shook his head. "She wasn't much for spending time in the kitchen. Cookies came from the bakery, and dinner most of the time consisted of takeout."

They quietly worked together until they had a couple of trays ready to go in the oven. Then they started over again. When they finally finished all of the cookies, he couldn't resist sampling one of them.

When he reached for a chai cookie, she lightly slapped his hand. "Hey, those are for tomorrow."

He frowned at her. "But how will you know if they are any good if I don't sample them?"

She sighed before pressing her hands to her rounded hips. "Go ahead."

He reached for one of them and took a bite. It practically melted on his tongue. He savored the infusion of spices. "Very good."

She smiled. "Glad you like it. Hopefully, everyone at the inn will enjoy them too."

He glanced at the time. "We have five minutes to get to the tree lighting." He stood. "Come on."

Her mouth opened, as though to argue the point, but then wordlessly closed. After she double checked that she'd turned everything off in the kitchen, she followed him to the door. They bundled up and headed out the door.

He told himself this wasn't a date, no matter how much it might feel like one. Because they were friends. Nothing more.

CHAPTER NINE

W AS THIS A DATE?

It sure felt like one.

Carol glanced over at Harvey as they stood in the small park next to City Hall. They'd arrived before the big unveiling. Even though it was cold and windy, there was a large turnout.

People didn't seem to mind the cold. They appeared to be warmed with the joy of the season as they smiled and greeted each other. Carol didn't see her sister, but she knew with Josie in charge of decorating the tree that her sister wouldn't miss this occasion.

In the background "O Christmas Tree" played over the loudspeakers. This was Bluestar's official kick off to Christmas. Only ten more days before the biggest holiday of the year.

The Christmas tree was shrouded with a big white curtain. Carol leaned over toward Harvey so he'd be able to hear her over the noise in the background. "Do you know how Josie decorated the tree?"

He shook his head. "It was a big secret. She was very excited about it. But usually, the tree is decorated with items related to whatever business is sponsoring the tree that year."

"Interesting. I wonder what that would be for an inn."

"When Melinda decorated the tree last year, she used miniature book ornaments as well as quotes from various books."

Carol remembered it. Melinda had done an amazing job. Since she owned the Seaside Bookshop, it made sense that she'd used a book theme. But Josie owned the Brass Anchor Inn. What would she do with that? Little bed ornaments?

Just then Mayor Banks stepped into the spotlight with a mic in his hand. "Welcome, ladies and gentlemen. I don't know about you, but I love this time of the year." He continued to talk while Carol searched the crowd for her family.

And then Josie stepped up next to the mayor. "My husband and I were thrilled to be chosen this year to decorate the tree. Lane really wanted to be here, but business took him out of town. Anyway, we hope you like it."

Josie handed the mic back to the mayor. "And now it's time for the big moment. Let's countdown. Ten. Nine. Eight... One!"

And then the curtain dropped. There was a ten- or twelve-foot tree. It was lit up with blue and white lights. It made it quite distinctive and very beautiful. White satin ball ornaments covered it. In between were brass anchor ornaments, painted seashells, and little seahorses wearing Santa hats.

"Josie did a wonderful job," Harvey said.

"I agree."

"Looks like decorating runs in the family."

Had she heard him correctly? Had he paid her a compliment? When she glanced at him, he was smiling at her. It gave her a warm fuzzy feeling on the inside.

And then her gaze settled on her sister. "There's Patty. I want to say hello."

"No problem. I'll be right here."

She thought about inviting Harvey to walk over with her, but she knew that would just stir up questions from her sister—questions she didn't want to answer. Because she couldn't help but wonder if Harvey was having a change of heart about them.

She wasn't ready for that. His brush off after his heart attack and then his cold shoulder this past year had her hesitant to trust him with her heart again.

ele

He had a hard time taking his gaze off her.

Harvey was surprised by how much he was enjoying the evening. He hadn't had this much fun since... It took him a moment to think about it. And then he was surprised by the realization that he hadn't had that much fun since they'd dated.

But this evening wasn't the start of anything. It was merely two old friends spending time together. Yes, that was it. Friends. Nothing more.

As his gaze strayed back to Carol as she approached Josie, he found himself once more caught up in her genuineness and warmth. When she smiled and then laughed at something Josie had said, the breath caught in his lungs. It wasn't just her appearance that was beautiful; she had a warm and generous spirit. He'd never met anyone quite like her.

"I didn't think you were coming to the tree lighting," Melinda said.

He turned to his daughter. "I wanted to support Josie."

"Then what are you doing over here instead of over there congratulating her?"

He brushed off the idea. "She sees me enough at the inn. Besides, she's busy talking to other people."

"I only see her talking to Carol."

He cleared his throat. It was time for a subject change. "Are you here by yourself?"

"No. Liam and Tate are around here somewhere. Liam saw Ethan Walker and wanted to speak to him. I told them I'd catch up with them."

Just then he saw Carol turn and start walking in his direction. His body stiffened. The last thing he wanted was for his daughter to observe them together. Maybe giving Carol a ride hadn't been such a good idea after all.

"I should be going," Melinda said. "I just wanted to stop by and say hi." She leaned over and pressed a feathery kiss to his cheek. "I'll talk to you later. Love you."

He turned to his daughter. "Love you too."

As soon as Melinda walked away, he turned to find Carol headed right for him. As she drew closer, he felt his heart beat faster. What was it about her that just a look could make his heart react?

"Was that Melinda I saw with you"

"Yes. She had to go. She was meeting up with Liam and Tate." He shifted his weight from one foot to the other. "Are you ready to go?"

She nodded, and they started to walk toward the cart. "I'm sorry I missed talking to Melinda. I haven't been by the bookstore lately."

"Oh yeah? What have you been reading lately?"

"A little bit of everything. I figure there's so many great stories out there, so why not try them all?"

"A little ambitious, don't you think?" When she shrugged, he said, "You must have a favorite genre."

She glanced over at him. "You really want me to choose just one?"

He nodded. "It can't be that hard."

"Oh, yes, it can." She pursed her lips, as though giving her answer a lot of thought. "I can only narrow it down to two."

"Fair enough. What are they?"

"Romance and cozy mysteries."

"Interesting. I don't read much romance, but I do read a lot of cozy mysteries. Right now, I'm reading: *'Twas a Murder Before Christmas.*"

"I just started it last night. So far, it's really good."

"I'm about halfway through, and I'm still not certain who the villain is. Every time I think I have it figured out, something happens, and I'm back to being undecided." He liked being able to talk about books with her. It was one more thing they had in common.

They continued to discuss the book on the short ride back to Carol's apartment. He insisted on walking her to the door. He was caught up in listening to her talk. He didn't want their conversation to end.

If she were to ask him inside for coffee, he would accept in a heartbeat. He told himself there was nothing wrong with them spending time together. They were just doing what friends did together.

They came to a stop outside her door. She turned to him. "Thank you for a wonderful evening."

"Not a problem. I..." Why was he holding back? "I enjoyed it too."

She gazed into his eyes. "You really did?"

When she looked at him like that, there was no way he could tell her anything but the truth. "Yes, I really did. How could I not? You make the most delicious pizza."

"I didn't make it. I only warmed it." She smiled at him.

"And the cookies were amazing."

"Hey, you weren't supposed to eat those." She sent him a playful pout.

"I only ate one." When she arched a disbelieving brow, he said, "Okay, two." When her brows rose higher, he sighed. "Okay. It was three. And they were the best Christmas cookies ever."

Just then there was a gust of wind. It rushed past them, sweeping a strand of Carol's hair into her face. His first mistake was instinctively reaching out to her. His finger moved gently over her cheek, catching the errant strand and then tucking it behind her ear.

As they continued to stare into each other's eyes, his heart pounded. When she looked at him that way, he didn't feel like the person who'd had a heart attack—the one who had to watch what he ate and keep track of his activity. When she looked at him that way, he felt like a thirty-year-old man again—ready to face anything the world threw at him.

His gaze dipped to her lips. The voice warning him that this was a mistake got drowned out by the pounding of his heart. He longed to once more feel her lips against his. He remembered them being as sweet as the sugar cookies she'd just baked.

Not giving himself time to figure out the right or wrong of it, he dipped his head and claimed her lips. For a moment, she didn't move. He was scared she might pull away, but then she kissed him back.

His arms reached out, wrapping around her waist and pulling her close. Her hands landed on his chest. In that moment, he couldn't remember why he'd been pushing her away—especially when she felt so right in his arms. It was as though she belonged there.

Deck the halls...

The ringtone intruded on their moment. He pulled back and reluctantly lowered his arms to his sides.

He shouldn't have kissed her. It was a mistake. And yet there was a part of him that didn't regret any of it. The memory of the kiss was something that would keep him warm on these cold winter nights.

Carol reached into her purse and pulled out her phone. She opened the door and then glanced at him. "Good night."

"Night." He walked away.

She pressed the phone to her ear as she stepped inside and closed the door behind her. He'd definitely messed up. As much as he enjoyed being around her, he knew nothing good would come of it. He couldn't offer her a lifetime of happiness, because he didn't know if or when he'd have another heart attack. His test numbers still weren't ideal.

The best thing he could do for her was to stay away. He didn't know how he would do that while she was working at the inn, but he would do his best. Because when he was close to her, he couldn't think clearly.

CHAPTER TEN

H E'D KISSED HER.

The memory made her heart skip a beat. The following morning, Carol felt like an excited schoolgirl again. She had no idea what to say to him. They'd said an awkward good morning, but after that she kept her back to the reception desk as she found a few small things she wanted to change with the lobby display. Probably no one would notice the slight rotation of a house in the village or the rearrangement of the figurines, but she did. And she needed everything to be perfect—or as close to it as she could get.

At times, she could feel Harvey's gaze on her. She resisted the urge to turn and look at him. She just kept working—kept second guessing herself as she tweaked this and that.

She felt as though she should say something more to him than just a simple greeting, but she had no idea what that might be. And when she glanced at him, heat rushed back to her cheeks. She wasn't the only one who'd grown quiet. Harvey hadn't said more than one word to her since then. It was a simple: *Morning*. It wasn't even a "good" morning.

In order to reach the ballroom, she needed to pass in front of the front desk where Harvey was working. She pulled out her phone and made a point of checking her emails as she walked past him. She was tempted to glance once more in his direction, but she resisted the temptation.

In the ballroom, she took a deep breath and blew it out. In here, she would be able to avoid Harvey. The tension in her shoulders eased.

The problem was the kiss was so good that she had a hard time putting it out of her mind. Still, Harvey's cool demeanor just now had her wondering if he regretted kissing her. The thought pierced her heart.

Shoving the painful thought to the back of her mind, she moved to the first shipping box. It was nondescript with a simple white shipping label. It was time to put up some special decorations that would match the theme of the room: a crystal Christmas.

Carol had sketched her idea of how the room would look when she was done. She decided to start with the Christmas tree because it was the most time-consuming task. She had ordered so many faux crystal decorations. The only question was which box held the ornaments.

She opened the first box. It held numerous boxes of icicle lights, as did the next box. She opened another and found ice cube men. They consisted of three ice cubes with cartoonish smiling faces, swizzle stick arms and little colored drinking glasses for hats. They were so amusing, and each one was unique. They were about twelve inches tall with twinkle lights within each of them that made them glow. There was a whole army of them to be the center pieces.

When she reached for the next cardboard box, she did a double-take. The box was bent up and part of the flap had been ripped off. She looked at the side of the box. *Wait. Is that a footprint?*

She gaped. *No. No. No.* This can't be happening.

She opened the box the rest of the way, which wasn't too hard. Inside were smaller white boxes that were also crushed. Her stomach plummeted to her boots.

When she opened the first white box, she found the frosted glass snowmen shattered. *This can't be happening.* She opened the rest of the white boxes. There were three snowmen that were totally intact. The rest were either destroyed or had pieces missing. Tears of frustration and disappointment stung the backs of her eyes. What was she going to do?

Her mind raced, searching for a way to salvage this fiasco. With her panicked thoughts, it was making it hard for her to come up with a reasonable solution.

She drew in a deep breath and slowly let it out. She'd start with the simplest solution. She reached for her phone and searched for the website of the company she'd bought the ornaments from. Trying to find a phone number for them was harder than she imagined.

At last, she found the contact number and dialed. She pressed the phone to her ear. Her call was immediately picked up by an automated voice with an impossibly long list of options. There was no selection for replacing damaged items. So, she selected Returns.

The phone rang and rang. Then another automated voice came on the line. "All operators are busy now. Please stay on the line, and we will get to you as quickly as possible."

"Come on," she muttered. "Hurry up."

She paced back and forth as the tinny Christmas music played. Every few minutes the annoying automated voice would come on the line and repeat the message about all operators being busy. She felt time slipping away, but she refused to give up.

Twenty-three minutes later—yes, she had timed it—a male voice came on the line. "Castle Mercantile. This is Archie. What is your name?"

She answered his many questions. It felt as though it took forever.

At last, he asked, "What do you want to return?"

"Actually, I want a replacement. My order is damaged."

"Replacement? That's not my department. You need to start over, and this time pick option eight. Make sure you answer all of the automated questions."

Wait. He wanted her to go through that long process all over again? *No.* She didn't have time for all of that.

"Thank you for shopping..."

"Wait!"

"Do you have a return?"

She knew better than to answer that question. Instead, she pretended not to have heard him. "Would it be possible to have a replacement here by tomorrow?"

"You would have to speak with the exchanges department."

"Archie." She used her authoritative voice that she hadn't used since her nephews were ornery little boys, and she was babysitting them, and they went wild with the garden hose. "I don't care what department you work in. I have a question you should be able to answer. What is the fastest your company would be able to get me a replacement order?"

"Uh..." There was the clicking of a keyboard in the background. "You want your entire order replaced?"

"Just the ornaments."

"That's a lot of ornaments."

"I know. How soon can I get more?"

"Uh..." There was more clicking of the keyboard. "I'm afraid that isn't possible."

Her heart sank again. "What isn't possible?"

"We are sold out of those items."

That wasn't possible. She needed them. She had no other ornaments to put on the tree. They couldn't be just any ornament. They had to go with the theme.

"Are you sure?"

"I am."

"Check again."

"But I'm looking at the inventory on my computer screen."

She wasn't willing to give up. Not yet. She lowered her voice and had a hard edge to her tone when she said. "Try again."

And so there was more clicking of the keys. He didn't say anything for the longest time.

When she couldn't take the silence any longer, she said, "You didn't find any, did you?"

"No."

The stinging of tears returned. She blinked repeatedly. She didn't have time to cry. She had a problem to solve. Too much was riding on this going correctly.

"I'll need you to refund my purchase," she said.

"That I can do." He sounded pleased that at last they were on the same page.

He had her email him a photo of the damaged ornaments and then told her she wouldn't need to return them, and then he processed the refund. She thanked Archie for attempting to help her and then disconnected the call. No sooner had she finished the phone call than she heard footsteps behind her. She turned to find Josie approaching her.

"Aunt Carol, I keep getting compliments on the lobby. People are in awe of the village you created."

"I..." She struggled to get her emotions under wraps. "I'm so glad they like it."

Josie's face lit up with a radiant smile. "I can't wait to see what you do in here."

"I can't wait either," she muttered under her breath.

"What did you say?"

"Um... I can't wait to see this room when it's finished." She just had no idea how she was going to pull it off.

"Can I help you with anything?" Josie asked.

Carol shook her head. "I've got it."

"After the holidays are over, you're going to be so busy with new clients that you're going to have a long waiting list." Josie's smile brightened. "You are so talented."

She didn't feel that way at the moment. She was afraid she was going to let her niece down. The thought made her stomach knot up.

"Well, I won't keep you," Josie said. "If you think of anything I can help with, let me know. Otherwise, I'm going to keep working on coming up with a very special gift for Lane."

"You don't have much time left to get him a gift."

"I know. But this is our first Christmas as a married couple, and I want it to be perfect."

"Good luck!"

"Thanks. I think I'm going to need it."

After Josie walked away, Carol moved back to the boxes with the destroyed ornaments. She picked up some pieces and tried to decide if there was some way to make lemonade out of a bunch of smashed lemons.

She racked her brain. No bright ideas came to mind. She randomly moved the broken pieces around. For someone who was normally creative, she didn't have one single idea to fix this situation. She sighed as she put the pieces back into the box. There was nothing useful to be done with them.

She was going to have to start from scratch. With so few days until the town descended upon the ballroom for some holiday festivities, she was going to have to create something special with what she found on the island. It was time to go shopping.

She grabbed her purse, turned for the door, and charged out. She was a woman on a mission.

CHAPTER ELEVEN

WHERE IS SHE GOING in such a rush?

Harvey watched Carol rush out of the inn. The frown on her face was evident. Was it because of him? He hoped not.

Maybe he should go after her. Although, he was pretty certain she wouldn't want his help. But seeing the distressed look on her face put his feet in motion.

He rushed out the front door without a coat. Oblivious to the cold weather with snow flurries in the air, he took long strides until he was a few feet behind her.

"Carol?" He watched as her spine stiffened, but she didn't stop. "Carol, wait up. I just want to talk."

She slowed and then stopped. She hesitated before she turned around. In that moment, he was struck by the overwhelming desire to wrap his arms about her, pull her close, and assure her that everything would be all right. He didn't know what the problem was, but he was certain if they put their heads together, they could find a reasonable solution.

When her anguished gaze met his, his heart lurched. He took another step toward her. His arms rose. His hands reached out to her. In a low voice, he said, "Carol, what's wrong?"

She took a step back. "It's nothing."

Her retreat was a stab to his heart. It was though she didn't trust him. The realization that she didn't had him lowering his arms. He didn't know why he thought she would want him to comfort her. Still, he couldn't just walk away.

His gaze caressed her face, taking in the stress lines bracketing her eyes. The worry shone in her eyes. And then he worried that it was his fault. "If it's something I've done, just tell me."

She shook her head. "It's not you."

That was a huge relief, but there was still something amiss. "Tell me what's wrong. Maybe I can help."

"You can't. I'm not sure anyone can. I've got to go." She turned and rushed off.

This time he let her go, but now he was more concerned than he had been before. What was going on with her?

After she climbed into her cart and drove off, he turned and headed back inside the inn. With the lobby quiet as the noon hour approached, Harvey left the newer hire to watch over the front desk. He didn't have a particular destination in mind. He just felt a driving need to figure out what had Carol so upset.

He ran into Josie in the hallway. Making certain to keep his tone casual, he asked, "Did you happen to see Carol?"

Josie glanced up from her phone and looked at him. "I did. She's in the ballroom. She did such an amazing job with the train and village in the lobby that I can't wait to see what she does with the ballroom." She smiled. "This Christmas is going to be amazing."

They'd come a long way from the frantic moment after the winter storm when the mayor had asked to use the inn to hold some of the holiday festivities. In the beginning, Josie hadn't been sure they would be able to pull it off, but now she was excited about it. Still, none of this explained what had upset Carol.

His thoughts circled back around, and he wondered if Carol had lied. Was she, in fact, upset because she had to work around him? But that didn't make sense. They'd been working around each other for days now. And they'd successfully been avoiding speaking to each other except for the obligatory greetings.

Was it the kiss? Was she expecting something more from him? He replayed their brief conversation. He tended to believe her when she said it wasn't him.

There was something else going on. And it appeared Josie didn't know about it. At least not yet.

Josie's gaze searched his. "Why? Is there a problem?"

He shook his head. "I just wanted to see where she wanted the incoming packages."

"I would put any deliveries in the ballroom." She turned her phone to him. "What do you think of this photo?"

He focused on her phone. There was a picture of her and Lane on the beach. He wasn't sure what he was supposed to say. "It's nice."

She drew the phone back to herself and swiped her finger over the screen. Then she held it out to him once more. This time there was a picture of them kissing under the mistletoe.

He cleared his throat. "It's nice too."

"Which one do you like better?"

He got the feeling this was an important question, and he didn't know what answer she was hoping for. "I don't know if I'm the right person to answer that question."

She frowned at him. "You're not the right person to give me your opinion?"

He swallowed hard. "Can I see them again?"

She showed him the pictures again. They were both nice pictures. He was a guy. How was he supposed to say which photo of them was better?

He'd never admit it to anyone, but he did a quick *eeny, meeny, miny, moe.* "I pick the mistletoe." Then realizing she'd want justification for his pick, he said, "After all, it is the holiday season."

She smiled at him. "It's the one I picked too. Thank you."

When she walked away, he breathed a sigh of relief. He was left to wonder what that bizarre conversation was all about. On second thought, he was probably better off not knowing the details.

His thoughts quickly returned to Carol. He couldn't forget the anguish that had been in Carol's eyes. What could have worried her so much? If it was something to do with the Turner family, he didn't think Josie would have been standing around in the hallway making a fuss over some pictures.

So, if it wasn't a phone call, perhaps it had something to do with the ballroom. Was someone in there who had upset her?

He turned on his heels and headed for the ballroom. He burst through the doorway and came to a halt. He scanned the room. No one was there. Maybe they'd left?

He let out a frustrated sigh. But who would upset her that much? He couldn't think of anyone at the inn who would do such a thing—not an employee nor a guest. And that left him without any idea of what was happening.

He walked farther into the massive room. It still had a new room smell. It was faint but it was still there. When Josie first had the idea for a ballroom, Lane hadn't been sure he was going to be able to make it happen because of town ordinances and so forth, but after a lot of back and forth with the town council, the expansion was approved.

Was it as big as some of the ballrooms in Boston? No. Was it bigger and grander than any of the other inns on the island? By far.

As he walked around the room, he noticed Carol hadn't started to put up the decorations. Could that be it? Did she feel overwhelmed? It was a very real possibility. By the number of boxes, there was a lot to do.

A lot of the boxes were already open. He pulled back the flap to have a better look. Inside he found... Well, he wasn't quite sure what he found. He lifted one up and stared at it. It was some sort of caricature. Were those supposed to be ice cubes? It had a goofy smiling face. It was actually cute. He was impressed that Carol had thought outside the box.

He returned the ice cube guy to the box. He wondered what else she had come up with. When he peered into the next box, he stopped. He looked closer. Were those broken?

He lifted out a smallish white box. Inside were broken pieces. It took him a moment to figure out what they were supposed to be. And then it dawned on him. They were snowmen. And the silver ties attached to the top hats let him know that they were tree ornaments—or rather they had been tree ornaments. Now they were ready for the garbage.

At last, he knew what had Carol so upset. Her plans had been upended during transit. But surely all of the ornaments weren't ruined.

He continued to search through the box. Most, if not all, of the frosted snowmen were in pieces. And trying to glue them back together would be a nightmare, if it were even possible, because some of the pieces were tiny.

There wasn't much time until the first event at the inn: Christmas Bingo. He highly doubted Carol could get a replacement shipment of ornaments in time. Perhaps they could collect various ornaments from people on the island or perhaps make them.

He knew who to call to help with this situation. He reached for his cell phone and placed the call. This just had to work...

─────ℓℓℓ─────

There wasn't much time.

Josie rushed along the sidewalk. There was still so much to do at the inn, but she needed to speak to Melinda. Every time she reached for her phone to call her, someone found her and needed something. If she wanted to have a conversation that wasn't overheard, she'd have to go to the bookstore. Plus, she still needed to pick out a book for Lane. In the evening, he'd take a book out on their deck, which overlooked the ocean. She loved that he wasn't such a workaholic anymore. The island was working its magic on him.

As she neared the picture window of the bookstore, she stopped to look at the display. Melinda liked to do elaborate window displays for the holidays. This year there was a snowman with a red scarf, a carrot nose, and a black felt hat. There were two penguins beside him and a squirrel in the paper tree in the background. Propped in front of the snowman and penguins were holiday-themed children's books. It was totally adorable. Melinda had such a great imagination.

As snowflakes began to fall, Josie moved to the front door. She swung it open and was immediately greeted with "I'll Be Home for Christmas" playing softly in the background. It made her think of Lane. Would he be home for Christmas?

Of course he would. This was their first Christmas as husband and wife. He wouldn't miss it.

It wasn't quite noon yet, but the bookshop appeared to be doing a brisk business. There were parents and children in the kids' section. Young and old alike were perusing the fiction section. And a few people were seated in the new reading nook area with hot drinks in front of them. They looked so relaxed. Josie longed to join them, but with the inn hosting Christmas Bingo in two days, there was a lot of work to oversee.

Her gaze moved to the checkout desk. Melinda wasn't there. Josie looked through the various aisles of books. She wasn't there either. But she did spot Ava Monahan, who helped out at the bookstore. She informed Josie that Melinda was in her office.

Josie moved to the back of the bookshop. The office door stood open. And she heard some giggling. *Giggling?*

She stopped at the doorway to find Tate playing with a fire truck. *Oh. Okay.* He made *vroom, vroom* sounds followed by *whee..., whee...* Josie could only presume this was his imitation of the truck's siren.

When their gazes met, Melinda sent her a smile. "What brings you by? Or do I already know?"

Josie stepped inside and shut the door behind her. You could never be too careful where small town gossip was concerned. If those gossips found out what they were up to, it would be over before they got Harvey and Carol together.

"Did you see Harvey and Aunt Carol at the tree lighting?" A smile pulled at Josie's lips.

"Actually, I didn't. When I talked to my dad, he was alone."

"That must have been when Aunt Carol came over to talk to my mother."

Melinda typed something on her computer and then pushed the keyboard away. "The tree looked amazing. You did a great job."

"After the tree you decorated last year, you really upped the bar for me. I was worried it wouldn't be unique enough. And then I was afraid I'd gone too far over the top."

Melinda waved away her worries. "You don't have to worry. I thought it was perfect."

"Thank you." Josie sat down in a chair beside Melinda's desk. "What did your dad say about Carol?"

Melinda straightened up some papers on her desktop and then glanced up. "He didn't say anything. And I didn't ask because I didn't want to make him suspicious."

"Oh. I guess that makes sense." Josie was disappointed. She was hoping by now that they would have patched things up. She brainstormed for a backup plan. Tonight's Christmas event was ice skating at the Apple Blossom Farm. "Do you think you can get your dad to go to the ice-skating party this evening?"

Melinda shook her head. "That's never going to happen. He doesn't skate."

"Oh. Maybe he could learn."

Melinda shook her head again. "I don't think so."

Josie nodded. "It's okay. My aunt's busy around the inn today. I'm not sure I could get her to go anyway. But we still have what?" She searched her mind to come up with tomorrow night's festivity. "The Christmas play."

Melinda shook her head. "I don't think there's much we can do with that. Unless we run into each other and have them sit beside each other, but I think they'll see right through that."

"Yeah. I suppose you're right." She couldn't help but feel her friend was too willing to find reasons the plan wouldn't work out. "So that leaves us with the Christmas bingo." She pursed her lips as she tried to figure out how to use that event to do some matchmaking. "Do you have any ideas for it?"

Melinda was quiet for a moment, as though choosing her words wisely. "Josie, I know you're trying to do a good thing, but maybe it just isn't meant to be."

She searched Melinda's eyes. "Do you really think we should give up?"

"I do. If it was going to happen, it would have happened by now."

"But they just seemed to be so good together. They were so happy."

"Josie, it's in the past. You gave it a shot to get them back together, but it didn't work. You're going to have to let this go."

She sighed. She didn't feel like it was time to give up—not yet. But she didn't want to argue with her friend, so she said, "I guess you're right."

Josie spent a couple of minutes playing with Tate and his trucks before she made her way back to the inn. She really thought she was onto something with those two.

It wasn't until she was almost back to the inn that she realized she'd gotten distracted and once more forgot to pick out a book for Lane. She sighed. She would have to make another trip but not today. She had too much work to do, and she hadn't given up on her matchmaking. Not yet...

CHAPTER TWELVE

CHRISTMAS SHOPPING...

Not exactly.

Carol was shopping, and it was Christmas time, but this manic rush through stores definitely had nothing to do with gift-giving.

She'd quickly worked her way down Main Street and popped into every shop that looked as though they had ornaments. To her disappointment, the ornaments were all picked over. It seemed the citizens of Bluestar were in great need of new ornaments that year.

She felt the weight of failure settle on her shoulders. The thought of letting Josie down made her feel worse. When Josie had offered her this job, Carol had assured her that she wouldn't let her down. And so she kept walking, kept brainstorming.

Maybe if she took the ferry to the mainland. It would take her the rest of the day, but if she worked throughout the night, she would get back on track. She stifled a sigh. Who was she kidding? She couldn't stay up all night like she had done when she was young. These days staying up till eleven was late for her.

She came to a stop. Time was running out. She had to make a decision and go with it.

It was then that she lifted her head and looked around. Right in front of her was the Lily Pad. It was a craft store that sold handmade crafts from local artists. Carol had visited it previously when she'd been looking for decorations for her new apartment.

If she recalled correctly, they also had a section in the back with a bunch of craft supplies. The more she thought about it, the more she liked the idea.

It wouldn't be as nice as the faux crystal snowmen, but it would offer a cozier vibe to the ballroom. People liked handmade crafts, right?

Perhaps it wouldn't hurt to go inside and have a look around. After all, she was there. She rushed across the street and entered the Lily Pad. The bell above the door jingled.

Lily Adams wore her hair short, in a stylish pixie cut. On her ears, she wore large hoop earrings. And her face lit up with a smile when she saw Carol.

"Welcome to the Lily Pad." Lily stepped out from behind the counter and approached her. "How can I help you?"

"Hi." Carol wasn't sure exactly what to say. She didn't want this disaster to make the gossip vine. She glanced around to see if there was anyone else in the store. She didn't see anyone.

She stepped forward and lowered her voice. "I'm thinking about making some ornaments. Would you have some supplies I can use?"

"Oh, yes." Lily gestured for Carol to follow her. "Come with me."

Lily led her to the back of the store where there were rows of craft supplies. There was so much more than Carol remembered.

Lily turned to her. "What did you have in mind to make?"

This is where Carol felt being upfront would be best. And so she explained about the ruined ornaments. "And now I'm desperate to fix things so I don't let Josie down."

"I'm so sorry that happened to you." Lily glanced around at the various items on the shelves. "You said you wanted snowmen, right?"

"Uh... Yeah. But I guess it doesn't have to be snowmen if you have something else in mind."

"To be honest, snowmen ornaments would be the easiest and fastest to create. And I just saw the cutest pattern to make one." She reached for her phone. Her fingers moved rapidly over the screen. A couple of minutes later, she turned her phone to Carol. "What do you think of this?"

Carol looked at the snowman with earmuffs instead of a top hat, a scarf and stick arms with felt mittens. The colors were pastels and very different from what she normally thought of as a snowman.

"I like it."

"Good. I think I have everything you're going to need."

"I'll need to make a lot of them. I have a very big tree to trim."

"Hmm... Maybe you need an additional type of ornament." Lily started to gather the supplies.

As Carol carried them to the checkout counter, she passed by some clear glass ball ornaments. She had a feeling she could do something with them. As she walked back and forth past them, a plan started to form in her mind.

"Would you happen to have some silver glitter?" Carol asked.

Lily looked over at her and smiled. "You've come up with another idea?"

"I have. I was thinking I could use these clear glass ornaments and create snowflakes on them."

"I like the idea."

By the time they gathered all of the supplies, Carol had to go retrieve her cart from the next street over and pull it up in front of the Lily Pad. There were just too many bags to carry in one trip.

At last, her cart was filled. Now she had to get the supplies in the inn without anyone noticing. Although, Josie was quite distracted with her mission to find the perfect Christmas present for her husband. But then there was Harvey. Other than earlier that day, he seemed to ignore her existence. As for anyone else at the inn, they wouldn't think to question her. So, it shouldn't be too hard to pull this off.

This evening was the ice-skating party out at the Apple Blossom Farm. She hadn't planned on attending, so she should have plenty of quiet time to work. And she was going to need every single second if she was going to pull this off.

Correction: she would pull this off. One way or the other.

ele

Her stomach churned.

Not quite an hour later, Carol stared at the instructions for the snowman, which Lily had been kind enough to print off for her. It seemed simple enough, but it was time-consuming. And she couldn't rush, because the ornaments had to look good; otherwise, there was no point in making them.

She removed the shipping boxes from one of the long tables. She'd spread out a cheap plastic tablecloth to protect the table, and then she'd assembled the first ornament.

She stared at the little Styrofoam snowman. It was cute. Was it cute enough to be deemed acceptable by Josie and the rest of the town? That was a question she didn't have an answer to, but it was too late to change course now. And so she continued to work.

When the door behind her creaked open, her muscles stiffened. Perhaps it was time to tell Josie the truth. She tried to take a deep breath to calm her rising nerves, but it felt like there was a tight band around her chest that wouldn't allow her lungs to expand.

She swallowed hard as she got to her feet and turned around. It was time for her confession. However, when she turned around, she got a big surprise. Instead of Josie approaching her, it was Birdie, Agnes, and the rest of the Purls of Wisdom. *What are they doing here?*

"Hello." Carol smiled. "If you're here to see the ballroom display, I'm afraid it's not completed yet."

"Actually," Birdie said, "we're here to help you."

"Help me?" In her surprise, she uttered her thoughts.

Birdie nodded as her gaze moved to the table. "I hear you need some help with the Christmas tree."

Now how had she heard that? *Lily.* It had to have been her because she was the only one she'd told about her Christmas disaster. Even though she was embarrassed that she wasn't able to pull off this job on her own, she was grateful to Lily for doing what she'd been too proud to do, ask for help.

"Thank you all for coming." Carol's vision blurred with happy tears. She blinked them away. "I'm not sure I could have pulled off making a bunch of ornaments by myself."

"Now you don't have to." Paige Maxwell sent her a reassuring smile. "You have us to help."

"What do we have to make?" Agnes Dewey frowned. Carol would have taken it personally, but after living on the island for a while now, she'd come to learn that the frown on Agnes's face was just her natural expression.

Carol swallowed hard. "I was just at the Lily Pad, and Lily helped me pick out a bunch of supplies." She went on to explain the idea for the snowmen and the snowflake ornaments.

Chairs were gathered, and another folding table was set up. More lights were turned on until the large room was brightly lit.

Carol couldn't believe how fortunate she was to live on an island with such caring and compassionate friends. No wonder her sister refused to move away from Bluestar.

The ladies chatted as they worked. Most of it was gossip. Harriet Pointer, who was a widow, was seen flirting with Frank Miles, a lifelong bachelor. This had been witnessed on two separate occasions in the past week. This apparently meant they were seeing each other. No one believed it would lead to marriage, because Frank was too set in his ways.

Carol didn't contribute to the conversation, but she listened. She wondered if they'd say the same thing about Harvey. Even though he had been married for years, he had now been single for quite a while. Did he like his solitary life so much that he wasn't willing to let anyone else in? Is that why he kept pushing her away?

"Oh, look at the time," Birdie said.

Carol found it was going on seven o'clock. How had it gotten so late so fast? She wondered if this meant everyone was leaving? She glanced at the collection of ornaments that had been set aside to dry. There were almost three dozen, but not enough to cover such a large tree. And they hadn't even started on the clear glass ball ornaments.

"It's time for the skating party," Carol said.

"Are you going?" Paige asked.

Carol shook her head. "I don't skate. But you should go."

"Yes, you should," Birdie echoed.

"I can't leave now." Paige glued the snowman's arms into place. "There's still so much to do."

"You don't have to worry about it," Carol said. "I'm so grateful for everything you've all done. But I've got it from here."

Everyone started talking at once. Carol couldn't make out what anyone was saying.

Birdie put two fingers in her mouth and let out a whistle. Everyone quieted down and turned to her. "This is what I think we should do. Paige this is your first Christmas in Bluestar, and it's extra special now that you and Grant are engaged. And I'm sure your little girl would love to go skating. So go ahead and go."

Paige hesitated, as though she was torn between staying to help them and going to have fun with her family. "But what about the other ornaments that need to be made?"

"Well..." Birdie said. "I'm too old for skating. And after my hip replacement surgery, I don't think my doctor would be too happy if I went skating." She glanced around the table at the other Purls. "Any of you going skating?"

The other ladies shook their heads.

"Can you all stay?" Birdie asked.

All of the ladies nodded, except Agnes.

Birdie turned to Agnes. "Are you staying?"

Agnes gave a dramatic pause before she said, "I better stay here. Someone needs to make sure you all don't get distracted with your talking and forget what you're supposed to be doing."

Birdie smiled. "Problem solved. Paige, you go and have a great time. You can fill us in on how Ruby does at our next meeting."

Paige profusely apologized for leaving early. She told Carol to call her if she needed any other help. And then she was gone.

Carol felt guilty that these wonderful ladies were giving up their evening to help her. "I really appreciate all of your help, but please don't feel as though you have to stay. I totally understand if you have other things to do."

Nobody left. And so they had burgers delivered from The Purple Guppy as they continued to work until eleven that night. By then, they didn't have all of the ornaments done. However, they had enough to make it possible to complete them the next morning.

"I don't know how to thank you all," Carol said. "I will make this up to you."

"There's no need," Birdie said. "Lending a hand is the Bluestar way."

Carol was so thankful to the Purls of Wisdom. With their help, she might just be able to pull off a refresh project that her niece could be proud of.

Chapter Thirteen

Eight days before Christmas

T HE MATCHMAKING WASN'T WORKING.

How could she have been so wrong about those two?

The next day, Josie woke up before the sun. She was in her office at the inn bright and early. When she paused for a coffee break, her thoughts strayed to Aunt Carol and Harvey. Josie had a knack of figuring out who belonged with whom. She'd never been wrong until now. Oh well, if Harvey wasn't the right man for Aunt Carol, she would find someone else for her.

In the meantime, she was starting to think she was going to spend her first Christmas as a married woman all alone. There was a legal issue concerning Lane's real estate holdings. He still didn't know when he'd be home. And she missed him so much.

She shifted her thoughts to something she could control—hosting Christmas bingo the next day at the inn. It would be the first big event at the inn. Everything had to be perfect. She couldn't overlook anything, no matter how big or small the detail. The inn was going to be on display for the entire town.

Josie made her way to the lobby. Harvey was working the early shift. Not so long ago, he insisted on working the late shift. He said after his wife died that he couldn't sleep, so he might as well do something worthwhile. Apparently, he slept well now because he never asked for the night shift.

"Good morning," Josie said.

Harvey glanced up from the computer monitor. When his gaze met hers, he sent her a warm smile. "Good morning. We got a fresh layer of snow overnight, but don't worry, the sidewalks and parking lot have all been cleared."

"Thank you." She stepped up to the registration desk. "I appreciate you going above and beyond to make these holiday events a success."

He waved off her words. "I don't mind. I know you have a lot on your hands with Lane out of town. Have you heard when he'll be back?"

She shook her head. "He's been dealing with problem after problem."

"I wouldn't worry. He won't miss spending Christmas morning with you."

"I hope you're right."

Just then he glanced away. His eyes widened ever so slightly, and a little smile lifted the corner of his lips. He kept staring off in the distance. Something or rather someone definitely had him distracted.

Josie turned around just in time to see Carol enter the lobby. She smiled and greeted them before moving toward the hallway. *Interesting.* When Josie turned back to Harvey, his smile was gone, and he looked like he was business as usual. *Very interesting.*

Once Aunt Carol was out of view, Josie asked, "Have you checked the ballroom lately?"

He shook his head. "I haven't. I don't have anyone to cover the desk."

Josie nodded. "I'll check on it." Before she walked away, she asked, "Are you going to the Christmas play tonight?"

Harvey nodded. "Melinda invited me. Tate's in the play, right?"

She nodded. "He is excited. He's going to be a star."

"I better go check on things for tomorrow night." She walked away.

As Josie made her way to the ballroom, she replayed that moment when Carol had walked into the lobby. She'd never witnessed Harvey so distracted. And then he had that little smile on his face. Oh, he was definitely into Carol. She had been right about them.

So, if it wasn't Harvey holding back, did that mean it was her aunt putting on the brakes in their relationship? It was definitely a possibility. Josie wanted to outright ask her, but she didn't think her aunt would be forthcoming. She'd have to figure out something else.

Josie opened the door to the ballroom. She stepped into the room, and she was surprised by the lack of decorations. Carol stood next to the Christmas tree. It didn't have any decorations on it either. What was going on here?

"Aunt Carol, why aren't the decorations up?" She tried to keep the worry from her voice, but she could tell by the frown lines on her aunt's face that something was amiss.

Aunt Carol approached her. "Josie, don't worry. I've got everything under control. And I have help coming today to put up the decorations."

There was so much to do and so little time. "Are you sure there's enough time to get it all done? The ballroom is a pretty big room."

"Trust me. I've got enough help, and I won't leave here until it's all done."

Josie let out a pent-up breath. "I'm sorry. With Lane stuck in California, I'm just a little on edge."

"But he'll be home for Christmas morning, won't he?"

"I don't know. I hope so." But she didn't want to think about Lane and how much she missed him. "Tell me what can I do to help?"

Aunt Carol waved off her offer. "Take care of your guests. And don't worry about this. I've got it. I won't let you down."

"I wasn't worried at all." Josie sent her a reassuring smile, even though she was still quite concerned. "Are you sure I can't do anything to help?"

"I'm positive."

Then she had another thought. "You're going to be done in time to go to the play this evening, aren't you?"

Aunt Carol hesitated. "Of course. I wouldn't miss Tate's debut."

"I have an idea. With Lane out of town, I don't have anyone to go to the play with. We could go together. That is unless you already have plans with someone? Maybe Harvey?"

There was a quick flicker of emotion in her aunt's eyes, but it was gone in a blink. There was something going on with those two, but she didn't know what it was.

Aunt Carol glanced away and busied herself by opening a box. "I don't have any other plans."

"How about we grab some pizza before the play?"

A moment passed before Aunt Carol nodded. "Pizza and a play. It sounds like a plan. Now I need to get back to work."

Josie glanced around. "Are you sure I can't do anything to help?"

"I'm positive."

Josie felt bad about turning and walking away, but she knew how stubborn her aunt could be. And she didn't want her aunt to think she didn't have faith in her abilities. Nothing could be further from the truth.

But she had one last idea to get Harvey and Carol together. If this didn't work, she was going to hang up her matchmaking hat. She reached for her phone and called Melinda.

ele

She'd barely said a word that morning.

Good morning. That was it.

Harvey was surprised Carol hadn't said more. He thought she'd at least say something after he'd asked the Purls to help her with the decorations. He'd been tempted to stop by the ballroom to check on the progress, but he didn't want Carol to think he was lingering around, waiting for a thank you.

Now that his shift was done at the inn, he was off to pick up dinner. He drove along the roads that had been plowed after the late-afternoon snow. With Melinda being pregnant and Liam at the school as part of the stage crew for tonight's play, Harvey had offered to pick up the pepperoni and pineapple pizza Melinda was craving. Just the thought of it made him cringe. He'd ordered a small mushroom pizza for himself. He wondered if it would be as good as the pizza he'd shared with Carol. In that moment, he missed her a lot. He'd been tempted to ask her to go to the play with him—as friends only. But he'd resisted the urge.

Bluestar was hopping that evening with people holiday shopping. Their arms were filled with colorful shopping bags containing goodies for under the tree. And when he reached the Pizza Shoppe, there was no parking anywhere near it.

He didn't have any other choice but to park a block away and walk, because he'd already called in the order, and Melinda was counting on him. He wouldn't let his daughter down, even if it meant trudging through a cold and snowy night.

And even worse, he'd forgotten his gloves at home. Stuffing his hands into his pockets, he set off toward the restaurant. As a frigid wind smacked him in the face, it felt like this walk was taking forever.

At last, his fingers wrapped around the cold metal handle. He pulled open the door and then stepped aside as a young family was exiting.

When he made it inside the warm restaurant, he found a lot of other people had the same idea for dinner. He took his place in the long line for pickup.

While he stood there, he glanced around the dining room, wondering how many familiar faces he would see. There was Bob Granger, Ike Thompson, and Fred Hanson with his wife. When he spotted Carol, his gaze lingered. Who was she there with? Her family?

She was smiling and then laughing. The breath caught in the back of his throat. She looked so beautiful. He wished he was the one who made her laugh.

"Next." A woman's voice drew his attention.

Harvey turned away before he could see through the crowded dining room to make out who she was with. He paid for the food but was told he needed to wait a moment for his order. He stepped off to the side so the next person in line could get their order.

As soon as he was out of the way, he turned his head. His gaze sought out Carol. The smile was still on her face. The crowd had thinned out a bit, and he was able to see she was dining with Herb Johnson, the groundskeeper at the inn.

Something uneasy churned in the pit of Harvey's stomach. He should turn away. Who she spent her time with was none of his business. And Herb was a good guy, though he didn't see Herb ever getting married. He was a self-proclaimed bachelor.

Perhaps he should go over and say hello. After all, he was friends with both of them. But his feet wouldn't move. And when she softly laughed at something else Herb had said, that uneasiness in his stomach amplified. His appetite fled him.

The woman behind the counter called his name twice before it registered that his to-go order was ready. As he made his way to the door, he wanted to glance back at Carol, but he didn't allow himself.

The truth of the matter was that he'd blown his chance with her. In fact, he'd blown two chances with her—once before his heart attack and the second was just the other day.

Had he been wrong to pull away after their kiss? His heart told him that he was an utter fool. But his brain said if he were to give in to his feelings for her, one or both of them would end up getting hurt. Not that it mattered now. She'd already moved on.

CHAPTER FOURTEEN

Seven days before Christmas

"WHAT EXACTLY HAPPENED LAST night?"

Early the following morning, Josie sat in her office at the inn with her phone pressed to her ear. She didn't have a chance to even say hello before Melinda blurted out her question. By the tone of Melinda's voice, her plan the night before must have had an effect on Harvey. *Good!*

Josie swallowed, and then in the calmest voice that she could muster, she asked, "What are you talking about?"

"When you asked me to have my dad pick up the pizza last night, I should have asked for more details about your plan. Because when he showed up at my place, he was all out of sorts. He was frowning, and you know that he's always in a good mood. He refused to stay and eat. Josie, this has to stop. But first, tell me what you did."

"Actually, I didn't do anything."

"Josie..."

She sighed. "My aunt and I stopped at the Pizza Shoppe last night for dinner before the Christmas program. My intention had been to invite Harvey to join us for dinner. You know, to break the ice between those two. But before he arrived, Herb Johnson walked in. So, I asked him to join us."

Melinda paused, as though digesting this news. "My dad saw you, Carol, and Herb having dinner?"

"Not exactly." Josie paused, not sure she wanted to tell Melinda this part.

"Josie, out with it."

Josie huffed. "Fine. When I spotted Harvey walk in, I made an excuse and slipped away. Harvey saw my aunt alone with Herb. They were having an entertaining conversation. The more my aunt laughed, the more your father frowned. If I had doubts about them before, I don't now."

"Josie, you said you were done with this matchmaking."

"No, you said that."

"Josie, this has to stop. If they find out what we've been up to, they will be so mad at us."

"Okay. You can stop lecturing me. I give up. It's up to them now. Honestly, I don't know what else to do, aside from locking them in a room until they work things out. You know, that sounds like a good idea..."

"Josie! Enough with the meddling. They are old enough to figure these things out for themselves."

"They're also old enough to be set in their ways and too stubborn to see what's good for them."

"But that's their problem. Right?" When Josie didn't immediately respond, Melinda said, "Josie, you're going to let this go. Right?"

With a big sigh, Josie said, "Fine. But you have to let me know if anything changes or if your father says anything about my aunt."

"I highly doubt that will happen. He's not that way, you know, to open up about his feelings."

"You never know." They belonged together. She just hoped they weren't too obstinate to see what was right in front of them.

"When's Lane getting back?" Melinda asked.

"I don't know. He was supposed to be back yesterday, but there was yet another business problem. I hope he gets home soon."

"I bet you do. I'm sorry he's away for the holidays."

"Me too. I sent him photos of Tate at the play. He was the best little star."

"Yes, he was." Melinda's pride echoed through the phone. "Even if he didn't have a speaking part, he did a great job."

Josie still believed this was going to be a great Christmas. She believed that her husband would be home any time now. She also believed Harvey and Aunt Carol would see what everyone else could see—that they belonged together.

She couldn't make any mistakes.

This was the big day. The inn was hosting Christmas bingo.

By lunchtime, Carol had the snowflake ornaments completed. Now they just had to dry completely.

She hadn't been sure about the handmade snowmen, but now that they were finished, she loved them. Instead of a crystal Christmas, the theme for the party would be winter wonderland.

She heard the ballroom door open. When she turned, she found Harvey entering the room. Her stomach quivered with nerves. Should she just ignore him? Or should she attempt to make light conversation?

Since she was never one to back away from a challenge, she stepped toward him. She forced a smile on her face. "Good morning."

His brows lifted. "Ah... Morning. You're here early."

"I am. Today is Christmas bingo, and I still have a lot to do before then."

He turned and looked around. He didn't say anything, but the surprise at the lack of decorations was written all over his face. "Can I give you a hand?"

She shook her head. "Thanks. But I've got it covered. Kent, Liam, Owen and some people from the furniture store will be here shortly to help with all of the lights and things."

He nodded as he stepped closer to her. "Do you have time for coffee?"

Her heart beat faster. She wanted to accept the invitation, but it was really bad timing. "I... I'd like to, but I can't leave now."

He nodded. "I understand. I'll be right back."

And then he was gone. She was left standing there, wondering what had just happened.

Buzz.

She pulled her phone from her pocket. It was Kent. He wanted to know if they should bring ladders. Since she didn't know how many the inn had, she told him yes. She already had one of their ladders to trim the Christmas tree. Speaking of which, she needed to get back to it.

With the lights wrapped around the tree from the top to bottom, she plugged them in. When they all lit up, she let out a pent-up breath. It was just the first of many challenges that day.

And now it was time to get those handmade ornaments on the tree. She hung ornaments over the fingertips of her one hand and then climbed the ladder. She carefully chose and placed each ornament. She repeated this process a few more times before she heard the door again.

Thinking it was her nephews, she called over her shoulder, "You're just in time to help."

"I'll be happy to help as soon as you have some coffee."

She gasped. She turned her head to find Harvey approaching with two coffees and a pastry bag in his hand. She was touched that he'd gone to such effort for her.

Her heart pitter-pattered. She knew she should say something, but the connection between her mouth and her mind had short-circuited. Was there a meaning behind his kind gesture? The knowledge that he'd gone out of his way for her made her heart beat faster.

When she went to grasp the ladder to climb down, the three remaining snowmen on her fingertips clattered together. *Oops!* She turned to the tree and hurried to hang them on the prickly limbs.

Free of the ornaments, she said, "I'm coming."

She rushed down the ladder. She was so anxious to see Harvey that she moved too quickly. Perhaps it was the fact that she was looking to see where he'd gone, or maybe it was the fact she'd leaned too far to one side, but the old ladder swayed.

She lost her balance. Luckily, she was near the bottom because she lost her grip on the ladder.

She started to fall. A cry ripped from her lungs.

And the next thing she knew, two sturdy arms wrapped around her waist. They lowered her safely to the floor. When she turned in his arms, Harvey stared into her eyes, making her heart flutter.

"Don't worry." His voice was deep and reassuring. "I've got you."

"Yes, you do. Thank you."

She noticed that he didn't readily let her go. In fact, it felt good to be held in his arms. Really good. As her gaze lifted to meet his, the breath caught in her lungs.

She never noticed how mesmerizing his blue eyes were. They were the shade of a clear summer sky. She could so easily let herself get lost in them.

Voices came from behind her. Immediately Harvey released her. He stepped away, but his gaze still held hers. It was as though there was something he wanted to say to her, and yet the moment had slipped away from them.

He cleared his throat. "I need to get back to the lobby. I left your coffee and a blueberry muffin on the table for you."

Without another word, he walked away. Her gaze followed him to the door. It wasn't until he disappeared from view that she was able to take her first full breath.

"Aunt Carol," Kent said, "where do you want us to start?"

It took her a moment to gather her thoughts. "I'm working on the tree. If you guys could work on the lights. The boxes are over there." She pointed to the other side of the room. "There's a sketch of how I'd like them. If you have any questions, just ask."

Kent nodded. "Hey, guys, we're working on the other side. We don't have a lot of time, so let's get started."

While they got situated, she moved to the table where coffee and a large blueberry muffin from the Elegant Bakery waited for her. She was touched by his thoughtfulness. But what did it mean?

———ele———

This was it.

Hours later, the big moment had arrived.

Carol had received compliment after compliment on the room. There were strands of twinkle lights draped across the ceiling. Icicle lights hung around the perimeter of the ballroom. The long lines of banquet tables were covered with white linen tablecloths. They were decorated with ice cube men, which would light up and twelve-inch skinny white Christmas trees with silver and blue ball ornaments.

On the floor near the back wall was a display of a snowmen family. There was a tall snowman and a snow lady as well as three little snow babies. Next to them was a red sleigh filled with fancy wrapped packages. In the background was a black lamppost wrapped in garland.

When Carol spotted Lily enter the ballroom, she made her way to her. Lily's face lit up when she saw her. "The tree looks fantastic." Lily gave her a quick hug. "I'm so happy that everything worked out for you."

"Thank you." She lowered her voice. "But I couldn't have done it without the help. Thank you for sending the Purls of Wisdom to help me."

Lily's brows scrunched together. "I don't understand. I didn't say anything to anyone."

"You didn't?" She was so sure Lily had been the one to spread the word.

"I'm positive. But I'm glad it all worked out. This place looks amazing." She glanced around. "And it looks like people are having a good time."

She'd thought the same thing. But she couldn't stop wondering who had told the Purls that she needed help with the decorations.

After Lily moved farther into the room, Carol looked around the room for one of the Purls. She didn't see them.

"Hey, Sis, you did an amazing job." Patty gave her a hug. "We are so lucky to have you working at the store."

Her sister's praise meant a lot to her—more than she'd expected it to mean. Happy tears stung her eyes. She blinked them away. After wondering if she would be able to pull this off, she was pleased with how it turned out.

Her brother-in-law George gave her a quick hug. "Great job."

Her smile broadened. "Thank you."

She got distracted talking to some more of her family. When they moved on, she noticed Birdie enter the room. Carol didn't waste any time. She made a beeline for her. She just had to know how the Purls had known she needed help the other day.

"Congratulations," Birdie said. "The ballroom looks amazing, and everyone seems to be having a great time."

"Thank you, but I couldn't have done it without you and the Purls. You all showed up at just the right time. How did you know I needed help?"

Birdie looked at her with her eyes widening with surprise, as though she expected Carol to know who was behind the plea for help. "It was Harvey."

Carol's mouth gaped. She struggled with the answer. She knew she should say something, but she couldn't find the right words.

Why hadn't she thought of him? Maybe because he had been sending mixed signals her way. She didn't know where she stood with him. But if he had been willing to get the Purls to help her, that had to mean something. Right?

"What is going on with you two?" Birdie asked. "With the way you two look at each other, I was certain there was something going on. Now, I'm wondering if I was wrong, which would be very odd. I'm always right about these things..."

"Birdie, would you excuse me?" Carol was already on the move before she'd finished her words.

She worked her way counter-clockwise around the room. Where was he? She couldn't imagine Harvey missing this big occasion.

Her search was slowed by so many of the residents complimenting her work. She made sure to tell them that the Purls had helped as had Lily. And then she realized there were more people she needed to acknowledge, from her nephews to the employees from the furniture store. She included Harvey in that statement. Now if only she could find him so that she could personally thank him.

She made it the whole way around the room, and he wasn't there. And no one had seen him.

Perhaps he was working the front desk. She headed for the door. She was almost to the doorway when Josie called her name.

Carol glanced over her shoulder to tell her that she'd be right back when she collided with someone. The breath was knocked from her lungs.

Large hands reached out and cupped her shoulders to steady her. She turned her head to apologize to the person she'd run into, when her gaze met the most mesmerizing blue eyes. The words died in the back of her throat. *Harvey.*

He stared into her eyes, causing her heart to pitter-patter. *Oh my!*

"I heard you were looking for me." He continued to hold her gaze.

Their physical connection was short-circuiting her thoughts. She struggled to recall why she was looking for him. When he released her and lowered his hands to his sides, she noticed the coldness where he'd just been touching her.

Able to think clearly, she swallowed hard and hoped when she spoke that her voice sounded normal. "I... I wanted to thank you."

He arched a brow. "Thank me for what?"

"Did you really think I wouldn't find out that it was you who asked the Purls to help me?"

Beneath his white mustache, a little smile lifted the corners of his lips. "Ah... So, you found out. I wanted to help, but I'm all thumbs when it comes to things like that." He nodded toward the tree. "The tree turned out amazing."

Heat warmed her cheeks. "As you know, I had a lot of help."

"Kiss! Kiss! Kiss!" A cheer started with one or two people, and soon others were joining in.

As she looked around, she found everyone staring back at her. Then Josie pointed above her head.

"Kiss! Kiss!"

Both Carol and Harvey lifted their chins and saw mistletoe hanging there. *Where had that come from?*

She didn't have time to consider an answer, because when she lowered her gaze, she found Harvey staring back at her. Her heart was beating so hard now it echoed in her ears.

"Kiss! Kiss! Kiss!" The collective sound of the excited voices vibrated through her body.

And then Harvey dipped his head. He was going to do it. He was going to kiss her. Her heart leaped into her throat. Her eyelids fluttered closed. And then his lips were there, pressing to hers. Nothing had ever felt more right in her life. He was the jingle to her bells.

A loud round of applause and whistles had them pulling apart. This wasn't supposed to happen in front of an audience—in front of most of the town. And yet it had. Now there was no way for Harvey to deny it had happened.

But when she looked into his eyes, there was a twinkle of happiness that she hadn't seen before. Had her kiss put it there? Hope filled her chest. As though Harvey sensed her question without her vocalizing it, he took her hand in his and gave it a squeeze.

His gaze met hers. "Are you ready to play some bingo?"

She smiled at him. "I thought you'd never ask."

CHAPTER FIFTEEN
Six days before Christmas

LANE STILL WASN'T HOME.

Josie told herself that it didn't bother her—that he'd be home as soon as he could. But now that her matchmaking efforts had come to fruition, and the town council had loved what her aunt had done with the decorations, she didn't have a distraction.

"Good morning, Harvey." She stepped up next to him at the reception desk.

His signature warm smile was back in place. "Good morning."

"Did you enjoy last night?" She wasn't sure how direct to be, but she really wanted to know if the evening ended well for both him and her aunt.

"I did." He turned to the computer and typed something before hitting *enter*.

"Aunt Carol was the belle of the ball. Everyone was so excited about her vision for the ballroom." When he nodded but didn't say anything, she continued. "Are you really going to make me ask?"

His gaze rose until he was peering at her over the top of his glasses. Confusion shone in his eyes. "Ask about what?"

She couldn't tell if he really didn't know what she was referring to or if he was hoping to avoid the subject. Uncomfortable with being this forward, she swallowed hard. "Are you and my aunt back together?"

He glanced away. A bit of color crept into his cheeks just above his beard. "We had a fun evening together."

"It's a start." She clamped her lips together. She hadn't meant to voice her thought.

He cleared his throat. "The bingo went really well last night, don't you think?" He didn't pause for her to respond. It was as though he were afraid she would bring up the subject of Carol again. "I think the mayor and the town council were mighty impressed. I can see them sending more business your way, especially now that you have the ballroom."

Josie smiled and nodded. "It has been a good addition."

"Any word on when Lane is coming home?"

"He thinks today will be his last day of meetings."

Harvey smiled. "That's good. Hopefully, we'll see him sometime tomorrow."

The inn's phone rang. She reached for it, but Harvey grabbed it before she could. She waited and listened, hoping it was a task that would keep her mind off missing her husband.

When Harvey hung up, she said, "What was that?"

"Just a guest asking for extra towels."

"Oh. Okay. I'll take care of it."

"No need. I'll message housekeeping." He reached for his phone to send the message.

Josie restrained a sigh. "Right. Okay. Do you need me to do anything?"

He paused as though giving it some thought. "No. I think everything is under control."

She couldn't go back to her house. She was already in danger of wearing a hole in the carpet from pacing. And she already figured out the special gift to give Lane on their first Christmas as a married couple. In fact, all of the gifts were wrapped and under the tree, just waiting for Lane to arrive.

The problem with running a well-run inn was that there were no problems for her to solve—no emergencies for her to overcome.

Oh, what a wonderful night!

Oh, what a hectic morning!

Carol sat in her office at Turner Home Furnishings. She couldn't remember the last time she'd smiled this much. Her office phone was ringing off the hook. Clients were signing up for refresh projects, and her calendar was full well into the summer.

But that wasn't what had her feet floating on cloud nine. Harvey had done that. First, with the mistletoe kiss and then afterward when he'd been so attentive for the rest of the evening.

She didn't know where this relationship was headed, but she had a really good feeling about it. Harvey was acting like he did when he'd asked her out for the very first time all of that time ago.

Now, she was thinking of investing in some mistletoe for her apartment. She might even keep it up year-round.

Knock. Knock.

She glanced up to find Kent, her nephew as well as her boss. She sent him a smile. "Good morning."

"It's a very good morning." He smiled broadly. "You really nailed it. People have been singing your praises since last night. I've even had a couple at the store this morning who picked out some furniture, and they insisted on having you do a refresh job on their living room. Imagine my surprise when I pulled up your calendar to find it filled."

She couldn't stop smiling. "People really liked the displays at the inn."

He nodded. "You did a fabulous job."

"But I had help..."

"But it was your vision. And that's what people are hiring you for. Keep it up and we can see about hiring you an assistant."

Her mouth gaped. She'd gone from worrying about keeping her job to the possibility of getting an assistant. *Wow!* This was an amazing Christmas. And it wasn't even over yet. There was still plenty of time to enjoy the holidays with

Harvey. And then they could ring in the New Year together.

"We'll talk more about it in the New Year." Kent's voice drew her from her happy thoughts.

"Sounds good. I'm just about to head over to the inn. Everything needs to be switched up for the seating for the movie this evening."

"I'll be over to help tear down the tables right after lunch. Mom and Dad are coming in to handle the store for the afternoon."

Carol nodded. "Sounds good."

Kent turned to leave. When he got to the doorway, he stopped and turned back. "Hey, happy looks good on you."

Happy felt good too. She told herself not to get too wound up in what happened with Harvey the evening before. He was just caught up in the moment. Nothing more. And yet it was too late. She was totally wound up in her hope for the future.

That kiss... She sighed as the memory played in her mind. He'd lingered when their lips had touched. It wasn't just a quick peck. There had been emotion behind it.

As she wrapped things up and shut down her computer, she told herself that she was going to play it cool when she arrived at the inn. She wasn't going to push things. She would let Harvey pick the speed at which they moved.

———~ℓℓℓ~———

Where is she?

Harvey found himself glancing up at the lobby door every few minutes, hoping he'd see Carol come walking in. He knew she had finished her work at the inn, but he was hoping she would come back and do some final touch-ups.

After all, tonight was the Christmas movie. He had no idea what title had been selected, but he had the sudden urge to watch it...with Carol.

Unless she changed her mind about giving him another chance. He wouldn't blame her if she said *thanks but no thanks*. But he really hoped that wasn't the case.

Harvey didn't have time to contemplate further, because the front door opened, and in walked some new guests. It was a young couple. They were hand in hand. The young man said something to make the woman smile. The woman leaned her head over on the guy's shoulder.

Harvey wondered if it was possible to capture a love like that at his age. Or was it asking too much? Was he too old for such a sweet romance?

He'd just finished checking in the couple, who were on the island for a couple of days to enjoy the holidays, when the door opened again. His gaze lifted and met the most gorgeous blue gaze. His heart thump-thumped. Maybe he wasn't too old after all.

The smile on Carol's face warmed a spot in his chest. She continued to stare back at him as she headed in his direction. He knew what he wanted to do. Well, there were a couple of things he wanted to do. Aside from kissing her, he also had a question for her.

When she came to a stop in front of the reception desk, she said, "Hello."

He had to get the question out there before he lost his nerve. "Would you like to go to lunch?"

Her eyes widened. "Now?" When he nodded, she said, "But it's not even noon yet."

He didn't know if she was letting him down gently or not. But he wasn't giving up yet. And it was almost eleven thirty. "This way we can beat the lunch crowd."

"But who will cover the front desk?"

"Did I overhear you need someone to cover for you?" Josie stepped up next to Carol with a smile, but the smile didn't go the whole way to her eyes the way it normally did.

"No," Harvey was quick to say. He didn't want to put any more pressure on his boss. "I've got everything under control."

Josie's gaze moved back and forth between him and Carol. "I'd like to work the front desk, so why don't you..." She paused as though to give it some thought. "Why don't you two go for an early lunch?"

Carol let out a nervous laugh.

Josie's gaze narrowed on one and then the other. "What's going on?"

When he didn't respond, Carol sobered up. "It's nothing. Harvey had just suggested taking an early lunch."

"Great minds think alike." Josie pressed her hands to her hips. "Now, get going. Enjoy your lunch and don't hurry back. While you're gone, I'll manage things here."

When Harvey went to argue, Carol gave a firm shake of her head.

Once they were on their way to lunch at the Purple Guppy, she said, "I'm worried about Josie. I think she's miserable without Lane and is trying to find anything and everything to distract her."

Harvey nodded in understanding. "I just can't imagine what's so important that he's missing the holiday festivities with Josie. All Josie says is that it's business."

"I'm sure it's very important."

"Agreed. So, what you're saying is that whenever Josie offers to help, I should let her?"

Carol nodded. "At least until Lane gets back. I have a feeling after this extended trip that he won't be out of town any time soon." She let out a little laugh. "Once they start a family, he won't want to be that far from home."

"That's true. I just hope he makes it home in time for Christmas."

"Me too."

By then they'd pulled onto Surfside Drive. The Purple Guppy was situated across the road from Beachcomber Park.

The building was painted a vibrant purple. It had large windows, which displayed the purple, black, and white décor of the dining room.

Harvey was able to pull into a parking spot right in front of the restaurant. Maybe there was something to this early lunch thing, especially when he had such a beautiful date.

When they went to get out of the cart, he said, "Stay right there."

He got out into the frigid but sunny winter day. He moved around the back of the cart, and then he opened Carol's door for her. He held his hand out to her to help her out. "Be careful. It's a bit icy out here."

She gripped his hand. When she stepped out, she slid right into his embrace. Her palms landed on his chest. He wondered if she could feel the way her closeness made his heart pound.

With his free hand, he reached out, wrapping it around her waist. "Don't worry. I've got you."

"You weren't lying when you said it was icy out here."

He offered her his arm and escorted her inside the restaurant, where the warmth wrapped around them. He hadn't been in the Guppy in ages. He glanced around, finding nothing much had changed. The huge aquariums were still situated throughout the dining room. The walls were painted light purple with cartoonlike fish on the walls.

There was a sign that said to seat themselves. He looked around. "Looks like you have your choice of tables."

"Let's sit over here by the window."

"Lead the way." He followed her over to a corner table.

His stomach was tied up in a knot. Last night, they didn't have much time to talk. There had been numbers announced, bingo cards to search, and a line of people complimenting Carol on what she'd done with the room.

But now, it was just the two of them, and he didn't know what he should say to her. Did he deal with the past first? Or was that too heavy for lunch? Maybe he was rushing things. Perhaps he should stay in this moment and just enjoy a meal with her.

He sat down across from her. "I haven't been in here for a long time. I wonder if their cheeseburgers and fries are as good as they used to be." It wasn't until he said it that he remembered his restricted diet. "Then again, maybe I'll have the salad."

He really did struggle with eating healthy. After a lifetime of eating what he wanted, he hated having to remove so many of his favorite dishes. But then again, that food was most likely what led him to have a heart attack, and he certainly didn't want a repeat performance. So, salad it would be...if they served salads. Maybe he should have checked before suggesting this restaurant.

"On such a cold day, I was thinking a nice hot bowl of soup might be nice." Carol sent him a reassuring smile.

The young server made her way to their table with two menus in hand. She took their drink order: two coffees.

Harvey was pleased to find that their menu included both soup and salad. Problem solved.

"Thank you for the lunch invitation," she said.

"I want to apologize," he said.

They both spoke at the same time. Their words blended and blurred.

"I'm sorry," they said in unison.

Then Carol let out a nervous laugh. He wondered if she was as uncomfortable as he felt. He longed for the easiness of the prior evening. But right now, there was no one to hide behind.

"You go first," he said.

"I've missed our... Our friendship."

Ouch. He'd thought what they'd shared before was more than friends. "I've missed spending time with you. I... I'm sorry about how things ended. I didn't handle it well after my heart attack."

"It was a lot for you. I'm just glad we're able to spend time together again."

"And Herb will be okay with it?"

Her brows drew together. "Herb?"

He nodded. "I saw you two having pizza together."

"You were there?" When he nodded again, she asked, "Why didn't you come over and say hello?"

"You looked busy, and I was picking up pizza for Melinda."

"Do you normally pick up food for her?"

He shrugged. "Not very often. But with her being pregnant, I want to help out."

"I understand. I was there with Josie." She paused as though she wanted to say something else but hesitated.

"Josie? I didn't see her."

"You must have been there when she went to call Lane."

"You'll probably think this is crazy, but do you get the feeling Josie has been setting us up?" He let out a little laugh. "I also think she's been conspiring with my daughter."

"Nooo..."

"Oh, yeah. I think so."

Carol smiled and shook her head. "Who would have thought my niece would be a matchmaker?"

"And my daughter? I guess they think we make a good couple."

Her gaze searched his. "Do you agree with them?"

This was the moment to let her know just how much he cared about her—how much he regretted pushing her away.

He reached out. His hand covered hers. "I definitely agree with them. I might have to get them something extra special for Christmas."

When Carol smiled, it lit up her whole face. Her blue eyes sparkled like an aquamarine gemstone.

And warmth swirled in his chest before working its way outward.

His heart thump-thumped. "Will you go to the movie with me this evening?"

Her smile broadened. "I'd love to."

"Then it's a date."

He had a feeling this was going to be a very special Christmas for the both of them. How had he gotten so lucky to have another chance with the most amazing woman in the world?

CHAPTER SIXTEEN

Five days before Christmas

D EFINITELY WALKING ON A cloud...

Even though Christmas had yet to arrive, Carol already felt like she'd received the best present of all—Harvey was back in her life. After worrying about everything from keeping her job to wondering if a friendship with Harvey was even possible, it had all worked out. *Merry Christmas!*

Lunch the day before had been wonderful. After they got through the awkward parts, they fell into a comfortable conversation just like they used to do before his heart attack. And the meal ended with Harvey insisting on picking her up to take her to the holiday movie that played at the inn. He'd been a perfect gentleman and insisted on taking her to dinner at Little Moon Hibachi Grille.

No matter how many times she told herself to slow down, she couldn't stop herself from falling head over heels for him. He made her feel like a young woman again—like anything was possible. It was so easy. He was so easy.

But she held back the words explaining how she felt about him. She didn't want to scare him off.

And there was a part of her that didn't trust he was in this relationship for the long haul.

She would wait for him to declare that this thing between them was something more than friendship. But she hoped he didn't wait forever to make up his mind.

"I really think you should be decorating the cookies." Harvey stood in her kitchen, holding a container of coarse red sugar. "You're so much better at it."

"But you're the one who signed me up for the Christmas cookie contest." She sent him a pointed stare. "And you didn't even consult me before you did it."

"There wasn't time." He sprinkled the colored sugar on the cookie dough. "By the time I got the idea, it was minutes away from the cutoff for signups."

A smile tugged at the corners of her mouth. It felt so good to know that he thought so highly of her baking skills that he just had to sign her up for the contest.

"I guess it could have been worse." She opened the oven and pulled out a tray of cookies. She set them aside to cool.

"What does that mean?"

"You could have signed me up for the gingerbread house contest. If you had, we wouldn't have gotten any sleep last night."

He paused as though giving the idea some thought. "I hadn't thought of it. But there's always next year..."

"Harvey! No." But her heart tap-danced in her chest to hear him talk about them being together in the future. Maybe there was a chance he felt the same way about her. Was she hoping for too much? Perhaps. But what was life without hope?

"Come on," he said. "You know you like a challenge."

She rolled her eyes. "Just keep decorating the cookies."

"Are you really going to make me do all of them?"

"No. I'm doing the ones for the contest. You're doing the rest."

He sprinkled some sugar on another cookie that was ready to go into the oven. "I suppose I can come clean now and tell you that I signed us up for sled riding too."

"Sled riding?" She was surprised. "Do you know how many years it's been since I did that? Then again, I don't want to think about how much time has passed."

He grinned at her. "And caroling."

"Well, that's not so bad." She arched a brow. "Wait. Do you sing?"

He shrugged. "I'll have you know that I'm a champion at lip syncing. Oh, and we're signed up for the ugly sweater contest."

She let out a laugh and shook her head. "So, what you're saying is that you signed us up for all of the remaining holiday events."

"Pretty much. Of course, there's still the Christmas Eve dinner. I didn't sign us up because I was waiting to ask you if you'd go with me."

She laughed again. "You signed me up for all of the other events, but you decided to ask me before signing us up for the dinner."

Was that a hint of color in his cheeks? When he raised his head to look at her, there was definitely a bit of pink stain in his cheeks.

"So, what do you say? Do you want to go to the dinner with me?"

"Well..." She dragged out her answer. The longer she took to answer him, the more distressed he looked.

"Carol..."

"Yes. I'd love to go with you." She grinned at him. "Now we need to get back to decorating these cookies. I think I'll make some frosting for some of the cookies. That way we'll have a variety to choose from to enter in the contest."

"Just so you know, you're doing the frosting." His voice held a firm tone. "I am not artistic."

And so, they continued to work together until there were dozens of decorated cookies. She'd already decided to take the extras to the store for the employees and shoppers.

Two out of three wasn't bad...

Josie was equal parts excited and relieved that holding the holiday activities at the inn had been a huge success. Everyone loved the Christmas displays, and she'd already had two families sign on for weddings in the coming year. And there were other groups that wanted to rent out the ballroom.

The only thing missing was Lane. The ten-day celebration was already half over and she still didn't know when she'd see him. She'd sent him photos of the decorations, but it just wasn't the same as him being there to see them in person.

Her gaze strayed to Aunt Carol. She was standing next to Harvey. He said something to her aunt that made her smile. *No.* It was more than a smile. It was more like she was glowing.

Josie's matchmaking had worked out. Who'd have thought? She might have a knack at this.

Buzz.

She reached for her phone. When she saw Lane's name on the caller ID, her heart pitter-pattered.

She turned on her heel and rushed out of the ballroom because it was so noisy in there. Hopefully, her husband was calling her to tell her that he had just landed in Boston, and he would be home in no time.

She imagined rushing home and setting up a candlelight dinner in front of the Christmas tree. Depending on how much time she had, she could make his favorite meal, chicken parmesan, or she could order takeout. It wouldn't matter, as long as they were together.

She pressed the phone to her ear. "Are you on your way?"

He laughed. "Hi. It's good to hear your voice too."

She noticed how he didn't answer her question. "You're still in California, aren't you?"

He sighed. "I am. I'm sorry."

Frustrated words rushed to the back of her throat, but she knew they wouldn't help the situation. And the very last thing she wanted was to end up in an argument with her husband during their first holiday season—even if they weren't together.

She choked down her complaints and smothered her pleas. Instead, she said the words from her heart. "I love you."

"I love you too. I promise I'll make this up to you. I never thought I'd be gone this long."

"You do know when you get back that I'm never going to let you go again." A smile pulled at her lips.

"Do you promise?"

"I do."

"Wait. You already said that part at our wedding." His voice had a teasing tone. "But just to refresh your memory, I do too."

She softly sighed. "I miss you so much."

"I miss you too. And I do have some news. My work is finally wrapping up. And I have a flight booked tomorrow afternoon."

"Yay!" Anticipation flooded her body. "You could have led with that news."

"And miss out on hearing how much you missed me? Never."

"I miss you. I miss you. I miss you."

He let out a hearty laugh. "I miss you more."

His words made her smile. Before she could speak, a cheer rose in the ballroom. It echoed down the hallway.

"What's going on there?" Lane's voice drew her back to their conversation.

"I think they're announcing the winners of the cookie and gingerbread house contests."

"Then I better let you go. Message me later and let me know who wins."

"I don't have to go," she said.

"But I do. I'm sorry. I love you."

She hated to say goodbye. "I love you more."

"I love you the *mostest*."

And then he was gone. She was left with the anticipation of seeing her husband in the near future. She couldn't wait. She didn't know it was possible to miss someone this much.

Josie made her way back to the doorway of the ballroom. A hush had fallen over the room.

Mayor Banks stood on a stage at the far end of the room. "The votes have been totaled, and the winners have been selected. First, I wish to thank Josie and Lane Johnson for the use of their wonderful inn. Let's give them a round of applause."

Heads turned in her direction as the clapping sound filled the room.

"Next"—Mayor Banks drew the attention away from her—"I'd like to thank Carol Carmichael for the amazing decorations in not only this room but also the lobby."

Another round of applause sounded.

"And now for the winners. I'll do the cookie challenge first and the winners of the gingerbread house contest second."

"Hurry up!" someone shouted from the audience.

"Yeah, come on," another person shouted. "We don't have all night."

Mayor Banks waved them off. "Okay. Okay." He unfolded a white slip of paper. "In third place, we have Mary Miller. Congratulations." He reached over and lifted a white ribbon and a white envelope from the table next to him. "You can come up and claim your prize."

A murmur spread over the crowd as everyone tried to guess who had won second place. There had been a seven-member panel of judges. Josie's mother had been one of those judges.

"And now for second place..." He opened the slip of paper again and closed it. His gaze searched the crowd. "The winner is... Carol Carmichael. Congratulations." He reached over to grab a red ribbon and an envelope.

Josie's gaze searched the crowd and found her aunt getting a hug from Harvey. A smile pulled at Josie's lips. It wasn't a perfect Christmas without Lane there with her, but it was still a very good Christmas.

CHAPTER SEVENTEEN

Four days before Christmas

A SECOND CHANCE AT life...

After his heart attack, Harvey had merely been existing—waiting for the next bit of bad luck to befall him. But Carol had showed him that there was so much life he had left to live. And with a grandbaby on the way, he planned to be an involved grandfather.

He had been spending all of his spare time with Carol. It was like they were both trying to make up for all of the lost time when he was struggling with his health complications.

In hindsight, he realized he was being such a fool to keep her at arm's length. She was the best thing to happen to him in a very long time.

This evening was sled riding. And he'd asked Carol to go with him to the Apple Blossom Farm. But first they were going to grab dinner at the Lighthouse Cafe.

When he stopped by her place to pick her up, she was ready and waiting to go. It was a good thing because they weren't the only ones who had the idea of having an early dinner.

They were able to get one of the last available tables. Even though he had wanted the burger and fries, he opted for the fish, baked potato, and coleslaw. Carol ordered the same, even though he told her that she didn't need to. She insisted she wanted it too. He was touched by her gesture. It warmed a spot in his chest.

After dinner, they drove south out of town. When they arrived at the Apple Blossom Farm, they found the sledding was already in full swing. Flood lights lit up the hillside. There were red, blue, black, and yellow sleds racing down the hill, while others were riding inner tubes.

As they stood there, Harvey realized his mistake. "I didn't bring a sled."

"No worries." Carol sent him a reassuring smile. "I see a bonfire over there. And a stand with hot chocolate. Let's go get some."

He knew she was just trying to make him feel better. "I don't know why I didn't think of it." That's not true. He'd been quite distracted that week. All he could think about was Carol.

"Hey, Dad." Melinda walked up to him and gave him a one-arm hug while her other hand rested on her expanding midsection. She turned and greeted Carol. "What are you two doing here?"

"Well," he said, "we were planning to go sledding, but I totally forgot the sleds. I should go back and get them."

"No, you shouldn't," Carol said. "We'll have fun without them."

Harvey glanced around. "Where's Liam?"

"Oh, Tate left his gloves in the cart, and Liam went back for them."

Harvey turned his head and watched as the sleds raced down the hill. There was a sheen to the snow. It looked as though the hill had more ice than snow. And those sleds were whipping down the hillside. Maybe sitting on a log next to the bonfire with Carol was the better option.

Just then a group of teenagers positioned their sleds at the top of the hill. It appeared they were going to race down.

Harvey glanced over at Melinda. "Where's Tate?"

"He's right here." She glanced down, realizing he wasn't there any longer. "Just a moment ago, he was running circles around me."

"He's over there." Carol pointed.

Tate was running as fast as his little legs would take him. Harvey's gaze moved back to the hillside. The sleds were already in motion. And they were headed for little Tate.

Harvey didn't hesitate. He took off at a run. "Tate! Tate, come back!"

He could hear people behind him calling out to Tate, but all the little boy did was laugh and run faster. Who knew a four-year-old could move so fast?

Harvey's heart pounded. His muscles strained. And yet adrenaline flooded his veins, fueling his pursuit.

Step by step he was closing in on Tate. It felt like everything was moving in slow motion. He reached out in front of him, hoping to catch hold of Tate's puffy blue coat.

And then a sled sailed past in front of Harvey. It was all he could do to keep from colliding with it.

Out of the corner of his eye, he saw Tate fly up into the air. Behind him a scream pierced his eardrums. He didn't have time to look back.

Harvey barreled forward. Tate ended up in a snowbank. When Harvey reached it, he couldn't see Tate. There was nothing but snow.

Breathing hard, Harvey paused. Tate had been moving with such force that he'd sunk down in the snow.

Harvey dropped down on his knees. He began digging. "Help! He's buried."

In seconds, people knelt next to him, and with their hands, they dug through the snow. And then he spotted a red boot.

"He's here." He dug faster.

When he was uncovered, Tate blinked and looked at them. Before Harvey could warn the boy not to move, Tate jumped up. He had a smile on his face.

"That was fun!"

Harvey felt a tsunami of emotions collide within him from worry to relief. Thank goodness the boy was all right.

"Help!" a female voice called out.

With Tate's hand within his hand, Harvey straightened. When he turned to find out what else had happened, he saw a group of people huddled around.

"Melinda!" Tate pulled on Harvey's arm.

The boy pulled him over to the group of people. Harvey didn't see his daughter among the group. In fact, he didn't see her anywhere.

Then the group parted, and there was his daughter sitting on the ground. Her hands were pressed to her baby bump. What was she doing on the ground?

Not letting go of Tate, Harvey moved to his daughter's side. "What happened?"

"I slipped on the ice." She rubbed her left side. "How is Tate?"

Harvey glanced at the little boy, who wore a worried look. "He's fine. I think he found it fun."

"Thank goodness."

"Melinda?" Liam rushed to her side and dropped to his knees. "Are you all right?"

While Liam, with his first responder training, examined his wife, Harvey stepped back. It was then that he noticed he was having a hard time breathing. It felt like his chest was in a vice, and someone was tightening it.

"Harvey?" Carol moved toward him. "You don't look so good. Are you all right?"

He couldn't catch his breath. "Take..." He took a couple of short breaths. "Tate."

Carol took the boy's hand. "I've got him. You should..."

Harvey pressed a hand to his chest as he stumbled and then sank down on the snow-covered ground.

Carol was talking to him, but he couldn't hear her. His heart echoed in his ears. His breathing was short and quick.

This was it. He was having another heart attack. He couldn't even help his daughter when she needed him. He was letting her down. He was letting down Carol. This is exactly what he didn't want to happen.

"Someone call nine-one-one." Carol knelt at his side. "It's going to be all right."

It didn't feel like anything was going to be all right. He hated seeing the fear written all over Carol's face. He hated even more that he was responsible for it.

Sirens.

Paramedics.

Life-flight.

It had all happened in the blur of a nightmare.

Carol was escorted to the mainland by Liam and Melinda. It felt as though the ferry ride was taking forever. She had no idea how Harvey was doing.

He'd been so pale when the paramedics had taken him away. She'd wanted to go with him, but there was no room for her on the helicopter. Instead, she had been left with her prayers for him to be all right.

Hours later, Carol and Liam stood next to Harvey's bed at Crossroads Community Hospital while Melinda rested in a nearby chair with her feet up. She was a little sore from her slip and fall, but she and the baby appeared to be okay.

And little Tate was no worse for wear after getting tossed into a snowbank. He stayed at home with Liam's parents. But he was disappointed when the sledding had ended so abruptly.

Carol glanced over at Harvey, who had been quiet. "Can I get you anything?"

He shook his head.

She was relieved to see he had color back in his face. And according to the machine he was hooked up to, his blood pressure was normal. They had all sorts of lines hooked up to him. They'd turned down the sound on the monitor so they didn't have to listen to the beeps.

A nurse had told them the doctor would be in shortly. That had been forty-five minutes ago. *Shortly* within hospital walls took on a different meaning than it did in the outside world.

Melinda was busy on her phone. Carol didn't have to ask. She knew Melinda would be communicating with Josie. Her niece had wanted to accompany her to the hospital, but there would have been too many people. Melinda had promised to keep her updated. Ever since they'd arrived at the emergency room, Melinda had been providing constant updates, which was difficult to supply since they weren't getting much information.

"You should go home." The words were spoken so softly she wasn't sure she'd heard them.

She looked at Harvey. "Did you say something?"

He cleared his throat. "You should go home."

She reached for his hand. His normally warm touch was cold, but that could have been because the emergency department was cold. She gave his hand a gentle squeeze. "I'm not leaving you."

"I mean it." His voice was soft but firm. "You should go."

He wanted her to leave? She felt as though he were putting a wall up between them. Her heart sank.

She'd thought they'd gotten past all of that, and they were going to stick together through the thick and thin. It appeared Harvey had a change of heart.

"Harvey Coleman?" A man in his thirties, wearing a white coat, stepped up to the foot of the bed.

"That's me."

"I'm Dr. Stewart." His gaze moved to herself and Melinda. "If you could give us a moment."

"It's okay," Harvey said. "You can say whatever it is in front of them."

The doctor gave a quick nod. "The good news is that you didn't have a heart attack."

"I didn't." Harvey's eyes shone with confusion. "But the chest pain and trouble breathing..."

"Tell me what was going on when all of this happened."

Harvey was quiet for a moment. Carol wondered if she needed to intercede on his behalf and relay the chaotic sceene. But Harvey found his voice and told the doctor about Tate's accident followed by Melinda's slip and fall.

Dr. Stewart nodded, as though he were taking it all in. "That sounds scary with a lot happening at once. I think what you had was a panic attack."

Panic attack? By the looks on everyone's faces, she wasn't the only one surprised by the diagnosis. They were all so worried about his heart that no one even guessed it might be this.

But this was good news. This was great news! Before she let herself get too excited, she asked, "So, everything is all right with his heart?"

"That is what I suspect, but I'd like to keep him overnight to run a few more tests."

Okay. She would be cautiously optimistic. When she turned to Harvey, he was still wearing a frown. She couldn't blame him. This incident had shaken both of them. But it wasn't enough to scare her away. She was in this relationship the whole way.

After the doctor departed, Harvey said, "Thank you for coming to check on me, but you should go home now."

Carol glanced at Melinda to see if she was anxious to leave. Melinda was still resting in one of the cushioned chairs. Her fingers were rapidly moving over the screen of her phone.

She turned back to Harvey. "We don't have to leave yet. We could stay until they transfer you to a room."

He gave a firm shake of his head. "It's getting late. You should go. I'll be fine."

She didn't want to leave him there. She got the feeling that even though the doctor had said all of the right things, Harvey was still upset over the events.

"Are you sure?" she asked.

He nodded.

"Can I get you anything before we go?"

"I'm good." And then his gaze finally met hers. "Thank you for being here with me."

Tears pricked the backs of her eyes. She blinked repeatedly. "There's no other place I would be."

When she bent over to give him a kiss goodbye, he turned his head. Her kiss landed on his cheek. She told herself not to read anything into the action. It was getting late, and he'd had a big scare. Everything would be better in the morning.

As they headed to the exit, she couldn't help but wonder if this had changed things between them once more. If they had—if he wasn't in this relationship the whole way—then she was done for good. She couldn't put her heart on the line, knowing if something bad happened that he was going to end things with her. It would be agony wondering when their relationship would implode.

CHAPTER EIGHTEEN

Three days before Christmas

F REE AT LAST...

After a long night in the hospital, Harvey had been sprung before lunch with a clean bill of health. He felt foolish for confusing a panic attack with a heart attack. Still, he was ever so grateful to be healthy.

But it also made him realize his health could deteriorate at any moment. All he had was the here and now. And he knew that he had to make the most of it.

He'd seen the fear in Carol's eyes, and he hated that he'd been the one to put it there. She'd been down a similar road when her husband passed on. Harvey didn't want to put her through that again. It wasn't right. She needed to find someone who was truly healthy and didn't have the threat of a heart attack hanging over their head.

He rubbed his forehead, where a nagging headache refused to leave him. He was certain he knew its source—the struggle over ending things with Carol. He'd never met anyone like her—so full of life and kindness. She made him smile—made him feel like the man he used to be. But this decision was what was best for her.

Melinda and Liam showed up at the hospital to pick him up. He couldn't deny he was disappointed that Carol wasn't with them. But she was just doing what he'd asked of her when he asked her to leave the hospital. At the time, he hadn't realized that her absence would hurt so much.

When they'd reached his house, he found his kitchen full of casseroles, cookies and cakes. It appeared his neighbors and friends had been up early, cooking. He was touched by the outpouring of kindness. There was no other place like Bluestar.

When he moved to the living room, he found Carol there. It appeared she'd been busy straightening up the place for him. More guilt heaped on him. She shouldn't be here, taking care of him. She had her own life to live. He knew she was very busy at work, ever since her Christmas decor at the inn had been a big hit.

"Welcome home." Carol sent him a big smile.

His instinct was to go to her and hug her, but he resisted the urge. He felt awful for holding himself back. He could see the confusion in her eyes.

He should end things now. And yet, he couldn't utter the words. After all, there were too many people around. This was something that needed to be done in private. At least that was what he told himself.

"Your fridge is filled," Carol said.

"You didn't have to cook for me."

"I didn't. I mean, I would have, but I didn't have a chance. I've been getting messages from people all day, wanting to know what they can bring you."

He grew uncomfortable having so many people fuss over him. And even worse, there was nothing wrong with him. He was released from the hospital and told that he could go back to living a normal life.

However, a little voice in the back of his mind warned him that although everything had worked out this time, it might not be the case next time.

"But I did spiff things up for you." Carol's voice drew him from his thoughts. "I ran the vacuum. And I found some clothes in the laundry, so I ran them through the wash for you. Is there anything else I can do for you?"

He was touched. Once again, the urge came over him to go to her and wrap his arms around her. And yet he held himself back. How was he supposed to end things with her if he was holding her—kissing her?

He had to think about what was best for her. The last thing he wanted to do was hurt her, but the sting of breaking up now was better than the pain of building a life together and then him having a fatal heart attack.

There was a lump of emotion deep in his throat that wouldn't go away. Why did life have to be so hard sometimes?

Realizing Carol was still waiting for an answer, he said, "No." His voice came out gruffer than he'd intended, so he rushed to say, "I mean thank you. You shouldn't have gone to such bother. I'm perfectly fine."

She smiled. "I didn't mind. And since you didn't need me at the hospital since Melinda and Liam were there, I decided to make myself useful. And you did mention where you keep your spare key."

He nodded. "I did."

Some people stopped by to check on him. It was a busy afternoon. And he welcomed the distraction because he still hadn't worked up the nerve to end things with Carol. He assured himself that he would do it later.

"Would you like something to eat?" Carol asked.

He shook his head. "I don't want to be rude, but I didn't sleep well in the hospital, so I'd like to lie down."

"Oh, yes," Carol said. "Of course. We'll get out of your way."

Carol, Melinda, and Liam rushed to get their coats and boots. He felt bad about asking everyone to leave, but he wasn't lying when he said he hadn't gotten much sleep the night before. He just needed to rest, and then the headache that had been plaguing him since he'd left the hospital would go away—then he'd be able to pick the right words to let Carol go.

"I love you, Dad." Melinda hugged him. "If you need anything, call me."

"I will. Love you too." He hugged her back.

"Do you need anything before we go?" Liam asked.

Harvey shook his head. "I think everything has been taken care of, but thank you."

They said goodbye and headed out the door to pick up Tate from Liam's parents.

Still standing in the foyer, Carol turned to him. "I could hang around if you want. I brought a book with me that I could read while you rest."

"I appreciate everything you've done." He sent her a smile. When she smiled back at him, his heart thump-thumped. Boy, was he going to miss her—even more than he did before. "But you should get some rest too. Isn't there caroling tonight?"

She nodded. "Would you like to go with me?"

"I don't think so. Not this year."

"I understand. Well, I'll talk to you later." She hesitated, as though she weren't sure if she should kiss him, hug him, or just leave.

He longed to pull her into his arms for a long hug, but he didn't allow himself that luxury. Instead, he moved to the door and opened it.

When she reached the doorway, she paused. Their gazes met and held, then she left.

He stood there, watching as she climbed into her cart. He waved and watched until she drove out of sight.

There was a wall between them.

Carol took comfort in the fact that Harvey hadn't broken up with her. Maybe it was just that he was tired. Yes, that was probably it.

Later that evening, Josie picked her up to go caroling. Everyone was meeting in the little park next to city hall. Neither Carol nor Josie spoke on the short ride. Carol knew her reason for being so quiet, but she was concerned about Josie.

She turned to her niece. "Is everything all right?"

Josie remained quiet, and for a moment, Carol didn't think she was going to answer. "Lane's flight got canceled. There's a winter storm in the Midwest, and it's snarled flights. I don't know if he's going to make it home for Christmas." She expelled a frustrated sigh. "I just don't know why he had to go to California during the holidays. Couldn't it have waited until after the New Year?"

"I'm sure he didn't plan to be gone this long." Carol knew the first Christmas as a married couple was special. She hoped Lane would find a way home.

"In the grand scheme of things, I know I shouldn't complain. We're very fortunate in so many ways. It's just that I miss him."

Carol reached out and squeezed Josie's hand. "It's okay to miss him. I'm sure he misses you too."

Josie nodded. "He tells me every time I talk to him." She glanced over to where people were gathering around the Christmas tree. "I think we better join them, or they'll leave without us."

And so, they joined the group. Carol's sister was there, waiting for them. Aster Bell was in charge of it. She passed out song books that were thin pamphlets as well as flameless taper candles.

They set out strolling up and down the streets of Bluestar. Residents opened their doors to them as they sang "Deck the Halls" or "We Wish You a Merry Christmas" or one of the many other songs in their booklets.

Carol enjoyed the sense of community and the smile that came over people's faces as they sang to them. The only thing missing that evening was Harvey. She wished he'd felt up to joining them.

But she'd done something she hoped would lift his spirits—she'd asked Aster to add his house to their list of stops that evening. Aster had been more than happy to comply.

They stopped at dozens of houses, including the Matsons' place and Birdie Neill's house. At long last, they ended up at Harvey's familiar house.

There were no porch lights on and the inside was dark. Maybe he fell asleep and forgot. *Yes, that must be it.*

They moved to the front porch and sang "Have Yourself a Merry Little Christmas." A minute later, the porch lights came on and the front door opened. Harvey stood there with a little smile lifting the corners of his lips.

After they sang "Silent Night," the carolers moved on, but Carol told Josie she was staying. Josie understood and told her that she'd talk to her later.

Once inside the house, she asked, "How are you doing? Did your headache go away?"

"For the most part." He stared downward.

There was something he wasn't telling her, of that she was certain. Part of her wanted to ignore the problem, but the other part said they needed to get whatever was bothering him out in the open.

With all of her winter gear still on, she stood on the rug by the door. She looked directly at him when she said, "Harvey, I know something is bothering you. Tell me what it is."

His gaze lifted to meet hers. He visibly swallowed. "I... I think rekindling things between us was a mistake. I can't be the man you deserve."

His words were like daggers stabbing at her heart. All along she knew it was possible he would do this to her again, but she'd foolishly thought their relationship had grown and was stronger this time around. She was mistaken.

He cleared his throat. "This time it may not have been my heart, but I could have a heart attack in a day, a month, or a year. I don't want you around when the worst happens. I... I don't want to hurt you."

The fact he was worried about her took some of the sting out of his words. Still, she didn't want things to end. She loved him.

"Harvey, I don't need you to promise me the future. I just need you to promise that we'll have here and now. One day at a time." And then she knew if she expected him to take a chance and really put himself out there, she had to be willing to do the same. She drew in a deep breath and released it. "I love you. I have since you first asked me out. I think we have something special. Please, don't let it go."

With her heart pounding, she turned to the door. Not waiting for him to respond, she opened the door and walked into the snowy evening.

She didn't know if her words would make a difference, but at least she'd said what was in her heart. If in fact they were truly over, at least she wouldn't be plagued by what-ifs, because she hadn't held back her love for him.

Her phone had been quiet. Too quiet.

Josie was concerned about her friend. A lot had happened in the last couple of days. And she hadn't had a chance to speak to Melinda until now.

So she took a break from the inn and walked to the bookshop. Along the way, she exchanged greetings with everyone she passed. The thing about living in a small town was that you got to know everyone.

When she approached the bookshop, she wasn't surprised to see an open sign on the door. Unless Melinda was put on bedrest, she would be at the bookshop. It was definitely a good sign.

She climbed the steps and opened the door. She was once more greeted by the scent of evergreen. Melinda must have a candle or air freshener with that scent. She loved the way it added to the holiday atmosphere of the shop. And if she wasn't mistaken there were even more decorations since her last visit.

She spotted Melinda sitting behind the counter. Josie approached her. "How are you feeling?"

Melinda sighed. "I'm doing okay. I got a bruise on my hip from the fall, but thankfully, that's all. How are you doing without Lane?"

"I'm fine." *Liar. Liar.*

"Josie, I know you aren't fine. Is there any word on when he'll get home?"

She'd just talked to him that morning. "He said he's trying. He's made it as far as St. Louis, but flights eastward are fully booked. He threatened to rent a car and drive. I told him with the winter weather that it wasn't a good idea. I don't know if he'll listen to me or not."

Josie didn't want to dwell on her problems or how much she missed her husband. If he didn't make it for Christmas, they would move Christmas to another day. They'd find a compromise and make it work. Just as long as he was safe. That was all that mattered.

With the bookshop quiet for the moment, they moved to the reading nook. They each got some hot beverages before having a seat at one of the tables.

Josie leaned back in her chair. "How's your dad doing? I gave him time off until after Christmas, so I haven't seen him."

Melinda sighed. "I think he's letting the panic attack really get to him. It really scared him."

"I bet. He was just getting past the trauma of his heart attack. He was starting to really live again. Is he still seeing my aunt?"

Melinda stirred her tea. "I don't know. I was at his place earlier but she wasn't around and he didn't mention her."

"Maybe she was working." Still, she couldn't imagine her aunt not fussing over Harvey, unless something had happened to come between them.

"Maybe." Melinda's voice drew her from her thoughts.

"But if not..."

"Josie, no." As though Melinda could sense the direction of Josie's thoughts, she said, "You've done all you can for those two. If it works out, it has to be up to them."

Josie sighed. "I know you're right. I just can't help feeling they belong together."

"I agree, but we can't make their decisions for them."

"Fine." She took a long sip of coffee.

"Do you promise that you're done meddling?"

Josie hesitated. "Yes. I promise." Ready for a change of subject, she asked, "Are you and Liam going to the ugly sweater contest this evening?"

"I hope so but Liam keeps going on about me staying off my feet after my fall. But it's one of my favorite Christmastime activities."

"Mine too. I was planning to beat Lane this year..." Her voice drifted away as she thought of her husband. *Please let him make it home safely.*

Chapter Nineteen

Two days before Christmas

S LEEP HAD ELUDED HIM.

Harvey yawned Monday morning as he set out on his morning walk. All he'd done the night before was toss and turn. Carol's words teased and tempted him.

Could the here and now be enough?

He kept walking. He couldn't sit around the house any longer. There wasn't even anything wrong with him.

Josie had been so nice to give him time off from the inn until after Christmas, but he didn't want it. If he ran the vacuum cleaner one more time, there wouldn't be anything left of the carpeting. Every dish had been washed, dried, and put away. And his bed had been changed, and the laundry had been finished.

The sun was out that day. There wasn't one single cloud in the sky, but the air was frigid. The snow on the ground wasn't in threat of going anywhere, but the sidewalks and roadways were all cleaned off.

When he reached the inn, it was a hub of activity. People were coming and going, many of whom were not guests of the inn. He knew what had drawn them—Carol's Christmas displays. They were beautiful and had so much character.

He actually had to wait to get in the front door. He'd never had to wait in line at the inn. He had a feeling that after this Christmas, there was going to be a huge boost in the inn's business. Josie was already planning to hire another front desk clerk and another person in housekeeping. At this rate, she might have to hire even more people.

When he finally made his way inside, he was surprised to find people were lining up to look at not only the train and Christmas village but also the display cases with the history of Bluestar Island.

He moved to the front desk to find Sara Chen working there. After she finished helping a couple sign in, she still had her head down as she entered something into the computer system. "Can I help you?"

"No. But maybe I can help you," Harvey said.

Sara's head lifted as a smile tugged at the corners of her mouth. "I'm so happy to see you. How are you feeling?"

"Good. Thanks. I'm ready to lend a hand."

Sara shook her head. "Josie said you're on vacation until after Christmas. She'd be so mad at me if she knew I put you to work."

"Yes, I would." Josie walked up to them. She turned to Harvey. "What are you doing here?"

He straightened his shoulders. "There's nothing wrong with me. And with all of the additional business, I thought you could use the extra help."

Josie shook her head. "We've got everything covered."

He looked over his shoulder at the people coming through the door. A couple waved. He waved back.

"Go home," Josie said. "But make sure you come back for the ugly sweater contest this evening."

He rubbed his beard. "I don't know."

"You can't avoid her forever."

"I'm not." His answer came out too fast and caused both Josie's and Sara's brows to rise. Lower and slower, he firmly said, "I'm not."

Josie patted his arm. "I don't think you believe that any more than we do." When her phone buzzed, she looked at it. "I'm sorry but I've got to go. And so do you. I'll see you for the contest."

Harvey turned to leave, but instead he found himself running into a friend from his school days. Even though it was a small island, their paths hadn't crossed in quite a while. They stood there, catching up on life.

His friend told him about the upcoming trip he had planned with his wife. It made Harvey think of Carol and how he'd like to travel with her. She would be great company. They could talk for hours, and he would never grow bored.

And yet he knew he couldn't promise her forever. The thought of her going through another great loss because of him made his chest tighten.

"I don't know what I'd do without Sharon," Ron said. "She's always getting me to try new things. Are you seeing anyone?" Harvey shook his head. Before he could say anything, Ron rushed on. "When you have someone in your life, you'll see. She'll have you doing things you never imagined doing. Be prepared for the swing dance classes."

Harvey let out a laugh. "I don't think so."

Ron arched a brow. "You laugh now, but wait and see..."

"Ron, come on." His wife gestured for him to follow her. "I want to see the ballroom."

"Coming, dear." Ron leaned over to Harvey and whispered, "Then again, maybe you're the lucky one by staying single."

Harvey knew his friend didn't mean it. He looked plenty happy as he strolled away hand-in-hand with his wife.

Harvey didn't feel lucky. He felt lonely without Carol to share things with. Like right now, he wanted to tell her about the conversation and ask if she would really make him go to dance lessons. She wouldn't, would she?

He walked out the door. He found himself realizing the reason he was struggling so much with this decision was because he was head over heels in love with Carol. He'd been in love with her ever since they'd started dating more than a year and a half ago. Now he had to decide what he was going to do about it.

ele

She picked up the phone for the hundredth time.

Just as quickly, she put it back down.

Carol had repeated this process many times. She was worried. If Harvey wanted to continue their relationship, wouldn't he have called by now?

She told herself she was setting herself up for a bigger fall by holding onto hope. She had to let him go. She somehow had to make peace with it. That was going to be harder because she couldn't deny that she was in love with him. The fact that she'd told him how she felt and he was still intent on ending things should tell her all she needed to know.

The problem with living in a small town on a small island was that there were no secrets. All too soon, the gossip would start. People would be guessing about whether they were dating or not dating. And some of the more straightforward people, like Anges Dewey, would just walk up to her and ask her point blank what was going on with her and Harvey. She didn't want to answer the questions.

And that was why she was planning to stay home this evening. She didn't want to go to the ugly sweater contest alone. It would be a constant string of questions of where was Harvey and how was he feeling. She couldn't endure that all evening.

The ballroom was set up. There was no reason for her to be there. Josie's staff would be able to handle everything.

Instead, Carol grabbed a carton of chocolate ripple ice cream from the freezer and a spoon from the drawer. She curled up on the couch. With the throw blanket draped over her legs, she reached for the television remote. She'd just turned on the television when her phone rang.

She was about to ignore it when a little voice in her mind whispered, *Maybe it's Harvey.*

Her heart fluttered with hope.

She grabbed her phone from the coffee table. It was Josie. Carol was tempted to let the call go to voicemail.

Immediately, she felt guilty. Josie had been so good to her. She'd given her an opportunity to show off her talent in front of the town. The job at the inn had secured her position at the furniture store for the next year. And most of all, she loved her niece.

Carol set aside the unopened ice cream and then pressed the phone to her ear. "Hello."

"Aunt Carol, can you come to the inn? We have a problem."

"What sort of problem?"

"The lights aren't working on the display in the ballroom."

"Did you check the outlet?"

"Yes. It's fine. We can't get it to work, and people are showing up for the ugly sweater contest."

"Okay. I'll be right there." Once she ended the call, she turned to the ice cream container. "Looks like our date will have to wait until later."

After returning the ice cream to the freezer, she changed clothes and grabbed her purse plus a small box containing spare lightbulbs. She rushed out the door. It felt good to have something to think about that had nothing to do with Harvey.

When she reached the inn, she found the place crowded. There were people everywhere. It appeared this was the place to be on this cold, blustery evening.

She rushed into the lobby and looked around. She was relieved to find the decorations and displays were as they should be. She headed for the ballroom.

There were a lot of connections to keep the lights on. If something got bumped, it was possible one of those connections might have come loose.

On her way to the ballroom, she got stopped multiple times by friends congratulating her on such a great job. When a couple of them inquired about booking a refresh job, she gave them her business card and told them to call her, and they'd set something up.

She wouldn't lie. The spiked interest in her work gave her a much needed boost. It didn't override the heartache, but it gave her something else to think about other than the huge mistake Harvey was making. Because some day he was going to realize what he gave up, and then it would be too late. She'd given him more than enough chances.

When she stepped into the ballroom, her gaze immediately went to the Christmas tree. It was lit up and looked fine. So, if that wasn't the problem, it must mean something was amiss with the snowmen scene. Carol weaved her way through the crowd to the other side of the room. And just as she'd expected, the lights were out.

"Thank goodness you're here," Josie said. "I didn't want anyone else to mess with it. I was afraid they'd break something."

"I understand. Let me have a look."

Carol made her way under the rope barrier and carefully moved to the area where the electrical lines connected. She tried this and that, but still the display wouldn't light up.

She went over everything she could think of, but still the display was dark. And then a thought came to her. *But surely it can't be as simple as that.*

She exited the ballroom via the service hallway and approached the utility box. She knew where it was because she'd tripped the breaker a couple of times when she was setting up the display.

And then she noticed the breaker had been tripped. That was really strange. How could it have been tripped? She hadn't changed anything.

The thought niggled at her as she reset it and made her way back to the ballroom. The display was lit up. Everything looked good. Now, it was time to make a quick exit.

"You got it to work." Josie smiled as she approached her. "Thank you."

"You're welcome." Carol thought of asking Josie if she knew how the breaker had been tripped. But before she could get the words out, she saw Harvey.

What is he doing here? Wait. Is he here for the ugly sweater contest?

The thought that he was there for one of the holiday activities after he'd just broken up with her hurt. It hurt a lot. It was like she didn't even matter enough for him to mourn the end of their relationship.

Hot tears stung the backs of her eyes. She blinked repeatedly. She refused to let him see how much this breakup was hurting her.

"Aunt Carol?" Josie's brows drew together. "Did you hear me?"

Carol drew her attention away from Harvey to focus on her niece. "Uh... What did you say?"

"I was saying that you better get started on your ugly sweater."

Carol glanced over her shoulder at the rows of people gluing all sorts of things from garland to seashells and everything in between to sweaters. Carol was disappointed she wouldn't get to see the finished products. People came up with some very interesting ideas.

"I... I don't think so."

Before she could say she was headed home, Josie said, "But you have to stay."

"I don't have anything with me to make an ugly sweater."

"No problem. We have supplies for anyone who needs them. We even have sweaters." Josie moved off to the side. There was a table with stacks of sweaters, baskets full of decorations, glue guns, glue sticks, and bottles of glue. "What color sweater would you like?"

Carol's gaze strayed to Harvey, then back to Josie. "I don't think so."

"What did you say? Red? Got it." Josie went over to the table and gathered the necessary supplies, as though Carol hadn't said a word.

"Josie, I don't think this is a good idea."

"Come on. You'll have fun."

She looked at her niece and realized there was no talking her out of this. Instead, she got another idea. "Is Lane home yet?" When Josie shook her head, Carol said, "I'll do one if you do one."

Josie smiled. "It's a deal."

CHAPTER TWENTY

H E KNEW WHAT HE needed to do.

Harvey was going to take the biggest risk of his life. He was about to put his heart on the line and trust in the unknown.

He just had to hope it wasn't too late and that things between them could be salvaged. He had to believe they would end up together by Christmas.

He set to work, grabbing the silver and red glitter. A bottle of quick-drying glue was next on his list. And for good measure, he grabbed some silver metallic snowflakes.

"What are you doing with yours?" Melinda asked.

"It's a surprise."

Her eyes widened. "A surprise, huh?"

He nodded. "Shouldn't you be working on yours?"

She nodded and then smiled. "Can't wait to see yours." Her gaze moved down the table to where Carol was working on a sweater. "I bet Carol would like to see it too."

That was what he was banking on. And so he got to work. This was the first time he'd ever decorated a sweater. He usually avoided these sorts of events. He'd picked the only blue one they had. He thought it would go well with the glitter. Then again, this was an ugly sweater contest. It wasn't supposed to go together. Not to mention, he wasn't technically competing in the contest—at least not the one for the ugliest sweater. He was competing for something much more important—Carol's heart.

"Only five minutes to go!"

Carol rushed to finish decorating her red sweater. Perhaps she'd been too elaborate with her design. She had to hurry, or she'd never finish in time. And once she started a project, she wanted to see it through to the end.

She reached for the hot glue gun and more green sequins. She glanced down the table to find Harvey working hard on his sweater. She couldn't help but wonder what his design looked like.

Just then he lifted his head, and his gaze met hers. They stared into each other's eyes long enough to make her heart pitter-patter. With renewed zeal, she rushed to finish the sweater.

"Three minutes!" Aster Bell called out. "Finish those sweaters."

Ugh! She was never going to finish in time. And so she rushed to get the important parts completed. Her hands moved quickly as she worked the glue gun. She ignored the fine strands of glue. She would clean it up later.

"Two minutes."

Her heart raced. She was probably making a big mistake with her design, but what was life if you didn't take a chance every now and then. She was going to put all of her cards on the table. Maybe she'd have a winning hand and... Maybe she wouldn't.

"One minute."

Carol's gaze moved over the sweater. It wasn't complete, but the meaning was there. That was what mattered.

She rushed to add some more red sequins. She worked rapidly.

"Time is up. Put down the glue."

Carol looked at her final product and sighed. She wasn't going to win any awards with it. Lucky for her, she wasn't aiming for a ribbon. She was angling for something more important.

Aster stepped up on the stage. "Thank you, everyone, for coming. I can't wait to see what you've designed. We're going to do the judging by age group. We'll start with the children ages five to twelve. Put on your ugly sweaters, and you'll get to show them off on this stage."

Carol knew it would be a while until her group was called. It'd give her sweater time to dry. In the meantime, she made her way over to the refreshment table, where there was coffee, cocoa, punch, and cookies.

She'd just grabbed a cup of hot cocoa and added some mini marshmallows when Harvey stepped up next to her. She should say something, but she didn't know what to say.

When they both reached for a peanut butter blossom cookie at the same time, their fingers touched. Her heart tap-danced in her chest.

When she raised her gaze to meet his, her heart launched into her throat. She yanked her hand back at the same time he pulled away. The cookie fell to the table and crumbled. She rushed to clean up the crumbs.

"Carol, I'm sorry."

What was he sorry about? The fallen cookie? Or was he sorry about the conversation back at his place?

Her gaze lifted to meet his once more. When she stared into his bottomless blue eyes, there was warmth in them. She felt her heart swell with love.

"Hey, Harvey, did you get roped into coming here too?" A man who looked to be about the same age held his hand out to him.

After they shook hands, both Harvey and the other man grabbed some coffee and talked as they walked away. Carol was left with so many questions and no answers.

The time had come.

And suddenly he was uncertain about this plan.

All evening, Harvey had been working up the courage to do this. Perhaps he should wait for a private moment. His nerves had him thinking it sounded like a bad idea.

But his brain said it was too late to back out now. He was the next one in line to parade across the stage in his sweater. He had it on under his winter coat. He didn't want anyone to see it until he was on stage.

He glanced around. He didn't see Carol. *Wait. Where is she? She didn't leave, did she?*

When Josie gestured for him to step up and show off his sweater, he shook his head. He couldn't go up there without Carol in the crowd. He told the person behind him to go ahead.

He felt as though his perfect plan was crumbling just like the cookie at the refreshment table. He didn't think she'd leave early. She hadn't even shown off her sweater yet. He got out of line.

Melinda came over. "What's wrong?"

He continued to look through all of the faces, searching for the beautiful one that made him smile. Was she in the ladies' room? Or did something come up with one of the displays?

He turned to his daughter. "Do you know where Carol went?"

Melinda looked confused. "I don't know." She craned her neck to look around. "She was here a little bit ago."

"I need to find her."

Liam stepped up next to them. "Find who?"

Melinda turned to her husband. "He's looking for your aunt."

"She left," Liam said as a matter of fact.

Harvey didn't need to hear more. He headed for the exit. His plan was a total bust, but that didn't mean he couldn't speak to her and tell her that he was a complete and utter fool.

He rushed out to the parking lot. He was about to get in his cart and head to Carol's place when he spotted her. She was speaking to someone. When she turned to go to her cart, he approached her.

"Carol, can we talk?" He braced himself in case she turned him down.

"Here?"

"Sure. I tried to talk to you inside, but we got interrupted. And then I had this plan to show you something important, but you left before I could show you."

"Show me what?"

He took her by the hand and led her over to a lamppost. She sent him a puzzled look but she didn't pull away. "What are you up to?

"This." He unzipped his jacket and pulled it back so she would see his sweater.

She read it.

She blinked to make sure it was real.

And then Carol read it again.

I love you. Here and now.

Happy tears pricked the back of her eyes. Her vision blurred. She blinked repeatedly. "You do?"

He smiled at her. "I do."

She opened her coat and let him see her sweater. It had a big red sequined heart with H + C in the center. A big smile came over his face.

When his gaze rose to meet hers, he said, "I'm sorry I reacted badly to the panic attack. I thought I was dying, and I didn't want to hurt you."

"But you're not going to push me away again. Right?" She desperately needed him to say that this time he would be fully committed to their relationship.

"If you're willing to take a risk on me, I'm in this the whole way."

Her heart was beating so loud that it echoed in her ears. She had to be sure she heard him correctly. "You are?"

"I am. I promise we'll face each day together."

"And you have my heart today and always. As long as we love each other, we can do this together."

He reached out to her and pulled her close. His gaze dipped to her lips. Her heart beat faster. As a few snowflakes started to fall, his head lowered. It was like one of those old black and white films where everything fades away except the two of them.

She lifted up on her tiptoes and pressed her lips to his. Even on this cold winter evening, his lips were warm and welcoming. Her heart beat faster. This was all going to work out.

Were they guaranteed tomorrow? No. But here and now would do.

His arms wrapped around her waist and drew her closer. Her arms wrapped around his neck. Her fingertips stroked through his thick snow-white hair.

Her fondest Christmas wish had come true. This was going to be a very merry Christmas indeed.

CHAPTER TWENTY-ONE

Christmas Eve

H E WAS ALL IN.

Now that Harvey had made the decision to open his heart and let Carol in, a sense of rightness had come over him. He didn't want to waste any more time, because he knew better than most that no one knew how much time they would get.

He felt as though this was the way it was always supposed to work out. With Carol by his side, they could face anything the world threw at them.

And now that it was Christmas Eve, he had a job to do. All dressed in red velvet with fuzzy white trim. Carol placed a hat upon his head. They stood in the hallway just outside the crowded ballroom.

She smiled at him. "You are the most handsome Santa."

"Well, thank you." And then in a deep voice, he said, "*Ho-ho-ho.* How would you feel about kissing Santa?"

Pink stained her cheeks. "There are people around."

"No one is paying attention."

She sighed. "You are incorrigible."

"Only where it concerns you." His gaze met hers, making his heart thump. "I love you, here and now."

"I love you here and now too."

Their lips met somewhere in the middle. Her lips were soft and warm against his. In some ways, the kiss felt natural, as though they'd kissed a million times before. Yet in other ways, it felt new and exciting. He hoped they had an eternity of here and nows.

"Wow..."

Their lips parted as they turned their heads and looked over to find a little boy staring at them with awe in his eyes. Perhaps Carol had been right about there being too many people around.

With great reluctance, Harvey released Carol, except for her hand. He threaded his fingers between hers and held on.

He turned to the little boy. "*Ho-ho-ho.* What's your name?"

"Tommy."

"Well, Tommy, are you ready for Christmas?"

The little boy with red curly hair nodded. "I want a bike for Christmas."

Harvey released Carol's hand as he knelt down to the boy's level. "Well, let's see here. Have you been naughty or nice?"

"Nice!" There had been absolutely no hesitation in his voice.

Harvey nodded his head. "Very well. I'll see what I can do."

The boy's gaze moved between Harvey and Carol. "Is that Mrs. Claus?"

Harvey glanced over his shoulder and caught the rosy hue staining Carol's cheeks. She looked so beautiful when she blushed.

He turned back to Tommy. "She isn't yet, but hopefully soon. Now you best go back inside and sit down. I might have a surprise for you tonight."

"Okay." He turned to go back into the ballroom. "Bye, Santa."

"Ho-ho-ho."

When Tommy disappeared inside the room, Harvey straightened and turned to Carol. She gave him a wide-eyed stare. Had his words caught her off guard? Hopefully once the shock wore off, she'd warm to the idea.

He leaned down and kissed her lips. "Come on. I have some anxious kids waiting for me."

"Oh, yes. Of course."

He picked up his big red bag. Lucky for him, it was stuffed with wadded-up paper and two special gifts. The gifts for the kids were already under the tree, waiting for him to hand them out.

He held his arm out to her. "Would you like to be escorted by Santa?"

Her gaze met his. There was happiness shimmering in her eyes. "It is very tempting, but I think I'll let you make a solo entrance. Just don't get used to it."

"Trust me. I won't." His gaze met hers. "Now you be good. You don't want to end up on Santa's naughty list."

And then he made his entrance to children's screams and the applause of parents. He had to admit it never got old playing Santa.

But this Christmas was going to be more special than any Christmas in the past. In fact, this holiday was going to be one of the best ever. And not just for him and Carol. A smile pulled at his lips. He had a special gift for someone else too.

He took a seat on the small stage. Josie was dressed as an elf to help him hand out the gifts. He loved watching the excitement light up the children's faces as he handed each of them a gift. *Oh, to be that young again.*

Witnessing the children's excitement, his heart filled with joy. The gifts were met with ear-to-ear grins, cheers, and the shy ones would get the slightest of smiles before they scampered away. With the parents' help, the children received a wide assortment of gifts from dolls to trucks and so many other toys in between.

Once he handed out the final gift to the last child, he said, "Does everyone have a gift?"

"Yeah!" The children's voices echoed through the ballroom.

"Are you sure?"

"Yeah!"

"Hmm..." He reached into his big red bag and pulled out a large envelope with a red bow on it. "But I have another gift. I wonder who it could be for." He held up the envelope with the name on it facing the children. "Any ideas?"

The kids shouted out various answers from "There's a name on it" to "Josie."

"Oh, wait." Santa pursed his lips as though considering the children's words. "I don't see a name."

"Turn it around!" the children said in unison.

He did as they said. "Now I see it. Is there a Josie around here?"

The children pointed to Josie, who was standing next to him.

He turned to her and held out the envelope. "This must be for you."

She pressed a hand to her chest. "For me?"

"You've been a very good girl this year. So, I have something extra special for you."

She narrowed her gaze as she cautiously took the envelope from him. She turned it over and looked at the name on the front, as though making sure it was actually for her.

"Go ahead," Santa said. "You can open it."

She ripped the flap open and pulled out a card. Harvey knew what it said because he was the one who had written it.

What you want most this Christmas is just behind the curtain.

Her eyes widened. "Really?"

"Go see." He let out a *"ho-ho-ho."*

A hush fell over the crowd of onlookers. She moved to the back of the stage on the left side and swept aside the curtain. There was nothing there. She rushed to the right side.

Josie pulled back the curtain and gasped. There stood her husband with a dozen long stem red roses in his hand.

When Lane went to hand her the roses, Josie rushed forward and wrapped her arms around him. "I didn't think you were going to make it back in time."

"Where there's a will, there's a way," Lane said. "And I definitely had the will."

Harvey turned away. He had one more gift—one more treat to make someone's Christmas extra special.

And so, he reached into his red bag and pulled out a very small package with a shiny red bow atop of it.

"Is there a Carol Carmichael here?" His gaze searched the crowd.

"She's here!" Patty Turner pointed out her sister.

"Carol, come get your present."

When she stood, he got nervous. What if she turned him down? By then she was making her way to the stage. It was too late to back out now—not that he wanted to.

He'd never been so certain about anything in his life. His heart pounded as he held the little box out to her.

———ele———

Her mouth gaped.
Her heart pounded.

She stared at the box in his hand. It was so small—too small for a sweater or a picture frame. It was just the right size for jewelry. More specifically, it was just the right size for a ring.

Carol's heart lurched into her throat.

Is it a ring? A ring. Oh my.

Carol moved on stiff legs. Nervous energy pulsed through her veins. She came to a stop on the stage. A hush fell over the room. It was though everyone was holding their breath, waiting to see what would happen next.

Harvey stood and then turned to her with the little black velvet box in his hand. "Carol Anne Carmichael, before I even spoke to you, I knew you were going to change my life. And even though it took me a while to see how our lives could intertwine, you didn't give up on me. You showed me love and patience. I love you and want to spend the rest of my life with you."

Happy tears rushed to her eyes. She blinked them away.

She couldn't believe he was saying all of these wonderful words to her. It was a dream come true. Each syllable, each endearing look filled her heart with joy.

Harvey, in his Santa costume, dropped to one knee. The breath hitched in her lungs. He opened the little box and held it up for her to see.

When she focused on the ring, she was awed. The large oval diamond was set between two smaller solitaires. They sparkled in the light.

"Carol, I don't know how many tomorrows I have, but I can promise you my love here and now. I will be your best friend to laugh with, your shoulder to lean on when you need to, and your safe harbor after a long day. Will you marry me?"

By now the happy tears dripped onto her cheeks. "Yes. Yes, I will."

Harvey pulled the ring from the box. He took her left hand and slipped the ring onto her finger.

He straightened and pulled her close. His arms wrapped around her waist while her arms slipped up over his shoulders. She lifted up on her tiptoes while he lowered his head. Their lips met in the middle. Her heart pounded so loudly she barely heard the applause and whistles.

When he pulled away, he took her hand in his. He led her from the stage, and they made their way through the inn to Josie's office, where he changed clothes. Once he was out of the costume, they headed to her place.

At last, they were alone. Carol kicked off her shoes and curled up on the couch with him. She held the ring out in front of her. It was true. They were getting married.

"Do you like it?" he asked in a warm, caring tone.

"I love it." And then she looked at him. "But I love you more."

He reached out to her, brushing his finger over her cheek. "I'm really sorry for what I put you through."

"It's in the past. This is the here and now. I... I just wasn't expecting this to happen so fast."

A look of concern came over his face. "Is it too soon?"

"Not at all." She meant it.

"I wasted so much time because of my insecurities that I didn't want to lose any more time with you."

"This is the best Christmas ever." She leaned toward him. "I love you."

He lowered his head to hers. "I love you too."

EPILOGUE

May... Bluestar Island

IT WAS THEIR WEDDING day...

Carol had been smiling since she woke up. She couldn't remember being this happy. And she wasn't the least bit nervous, because she was certain they belonged together. Okay, maybe she was a little nervous that she would forget something and mess up this perfect day.

So far, she'd done well. With the wedding march being played on the church organ, she'd made it to the front of the church without tripping. And now with Harvey holding her hands, she felt reassured that everything was going to work out just the way it was meant to.

"The bride and groom have a few words they've written for each other." The pastor took a step back and let them have this moment.

Carol looked at Harvey in his new dark suit and tie. He looked so dashing, so sweet, and so loving. How had she gotten so lucky?

They'd already agreed that he should go first. She expected him to let go of her hands so he could put on his reading glasses and pull a slip of paper from his pocket, but he did none of that.

Instead, he stared deep into her eyes. "Carol, I knew from the very first time I asked you out that you were going to change my life. I just wonder if you know how much marrying me is going to change yours."

She had absolutely no idea where he was going with this. But she had to admit that she was intrigued.

He cleared his throat. "From now on, you'll be known as Mrs. Claus." A soft laughter filled the church. "And you're going to be known by two adorable little ones as Nana."

Happy tears gathered in her eyes. Her heart was so full of love that it was overflowing. She blinked repeatedly, trying to keep the tears in check so she wouldn't ruin her makeup for the photos, but she was fighting a losing battle.

"You also owe me a date sled riding next Christmas, and I intend to collect. You are my best friend, and I can't wait to share new adventures with you. I love you."

She couldn't wait either. She leaned forward and lifted up on her tiptoes to press a kiss to his lips. Those were the sweetest words.

When she pulled back, she tried to remember her words for him. And she failed. She swiped at the happy tears on her cheeks. Then she reached into one of the pockets in her dress and pulled out her reading glasses. Thank goodness she'd picked out the pale pink, knee-length dress with pockets. Who knew those pockets were going to be so important?

With her glasses on, she pulled a slip of paper from her other pocket. She gazed up at him. "This is your fault. I had everything memorized, but then you said those sweet words and everything went straight out of my head."

Her heart was thumping and her hands trembled as she unfolded the paper. She couldn't mess this up. It was too important.

"Harvey, our path hasn't been a straight one. It had a few twists and turns. In the end, I wouldn't change any of it, because I think this journey made us stronger and showed us there isn't anything we can't face together. Because I am here for you always. We don't know what the future has in store, but I promise to love you here and now... And for always."

He leaned forward. "And I love you here and now... And for always."

"I think that's my cue," the pastor said. He walked them through the rest of the ceremony. At the end, he said, "You may kiss your bride."

Harvey didn't waste any time sweeping her up in his embrace and kissing her. It wasn't just a little peck. Not even close. He kissed her thoroughly until her toes felt as though they'd left the floor.

When he released her, he held his arm out to her. "Shall we, Mrs. Coleman?"

She placed her hand in the crook of his arm. "Yes, we shall, Mr. Coleman."

They smiled at each other before they walked down the aisle past a church full of smiling family and friends. Talk about a dream wedding...

The now Mrs. Carol Coleman couldn't have imagined the day being any better. When they stepped outside, the sun was bright and warmed her face. There was a gentle breeze that carried the soft scent of lilacs.

She glanced over at her groom. Harvey had been a perfect gentleman the entire day. Although she had to admit when she saw that he'd shaved his beard and mustache, she was caught off guard. He hadn't warned her he was doing it, so it came as quite a surprise when she was walking down the aisle. Without his beard, he looked at least ten years younger. She teased him about marrying a younger man. He asked if she would still have him. She told him there was no way she was letting him get away.

As they stood outside the church that had just been repaired after the Christmastime ice storm, she turned to Harvey. "Are you truly happy?"

"That's a silly question to ask a man on his wedding day." He wrapped his arms around her waist and pulled her close. "I can't remember being this happy. Are you happy?"

"More than I can put in words."

He leaned down and gave her a light kiss on the lips. It made her heart flutter.

When they parted, she spotted their guests exiting the church. Everyone was headed to the Brass Anchor Inn for the reception in the ballroom. Carol couldn't wait to dance with her groom. She loved to dance, and to her surprise, Harvey was light on his feet.

Out of the corner of her eye, she spotted a young woman with short dark hair in a robin's egg–blue dress. Carol didn't recognize her. She must have been someone on Harvey's guest list. As the woman was coming down the steps, she suddenly glanced up right as her foot slipped over the edge of a step. She fell forward.

Carol gasped. But she was too far away to come to the young woman's aid. And then a man stepped in, catching the woman. It took Carol a moment to realize it was Owen. Thank goodness he was close by.

"What's the matter?" Harvey asked.

"Um… Nothing." Carol continued to watch as the young lady thanked Owen.

The woman's cheeks pinkened, and her eyes sparkled as she looked at Owen. Carol didn't miss how Owen lingered by the woman's side just a moment longer than was necessary. Was it possible Owen had at last found someone he was interested in?

Owen was the youngest of her sister's children and final remaining bachelor. He was a bit of a hermit with those digital games he designed for a living. Maybe this wedding was just what he needed to find that special someone. Perhaps he already had…

Carol wondered who the woman was. Her gaze searched for the young woman in the pretty dress so she could point her out to Harvey. Maybe he would be able to fill her in on her name, but the mystery woman had already disappeared from view. Carol sighed.

"Are you ready to go party until the sun comes up?" Harvey's voice drew her from her thoughts.

"You've got to be kidding?" He was kidding, wasn't he? Her gaze searched his, not quite sure. "I... I can't do an all-nighter. How old do you think I am?"

Harvey let out a laugh. "How about we dance until our feet hurt?"

"Now you're talking my language." She smiled at her husband. "I love you, Mr. Coleman."

"I love you, Mrs. Coleman."

He held out his hand to her. She placed hers in his. Their fingers laced together. Together they walked to Harvey's cart, which had been decorated by some unknown guests, who were most likely her niece and nephews. There were white streamers, balloons, and a sign that hung on the back that read: *Just Married. Perfect.* Her gaze moved to her husband, and she smiled. *Absolutely perfect.*

Keep reading Carol and Harvey's story! Sign up for my newsletter and receive not one but TWO bonus scenes:

- **Get your bonus epilogue HERE.**

- **And read about Melinda and Liam's baby HERE.**

And then return to Bluestar Island for the final book in The Turner Family of Bluestar

Island series... **RACE TO THE BEACH.** The Bluestar Hospital is set to open that summer, and it will bring Maxi and Owen together...as rivals in the vintage grand prix!

Carol's Chai Spice Cookies

Ingredients:

- 8 oz Cream Cheese, softened
- ¾ cup unsalted butter, softened
- 1 cup sugar
- 3 tsp vanilla
- 2 ¼ cups flour
- ½ tsp baking soda
- 3 tsp chai spice mix powder
- ½ cup pecans pieces
- 1 cup powdered sugar

· Preheat oven to 350°F
· Line baking sheets with parchment paper.

- In small bowl, coarsely chop pecan halves. Set aside.
- In large bowl, beat cream cheese, butter, sugar and vanilla until well blended.
- Add baking soda. Blend.
- Add 2 tsp Chai mix powder. Blend.
- Slowly add flour, blending after each small addition until all flour is blended.
- Add pecan pieces. Mix by hand.
- Refrigerate until chilled, an hour minimum.
- Roll dough into one-inch balls.
- Using palms, flatten the ball slightly. Place on baking sheet, leaving 1 inch spacing.
- Bake for approximately 14 minutes.
- In a small dish, mix 1 cup powdered sugar and the remaining tsp of chai mix.
- Cool cookies for 5 minutes.
- Roll cookie in the powder sugar mix and then place on cooling rack.
- Store in a Ziploc bag or other sealed container.

Enjoy!

Afterword

Thanks so much for reading Carol and Harvey's story. I hope their journey made your heart smile. If you did enjoy the book, please consider...

- Help spreading the word about A BRASS ANCHOR INN CHRISTMAS by writing a review.
- Subscribe to my newsletter in order to receive information about my next release as well as find out about giveaways and special sales.
- You can like my author page on Facebook or follow me on Twitter.

I hope you'll come back to Bluestar Island and read the continuing adventures of its residents. In upcoming books, there will be updates on previous couples as well as the addition of some new visitors to the islander.

Coming next is Maxi & Owen's story in RACE TO THE BEACH.

Thanks again for your support! It is HUGELY appreciated.

Happy reading,
Jennifer

ABOUT AUTHOR

Award-winning author, Jennifer Faye pens fun, heartwarming contemporary romances. With more than a million books sold, she is internationally published with books translated into more than a dozen languages and her work has been optioned for film. She is a two-time winner of the RT Book Reviews Reviewers' Choice Award, the CataRomance Reviewers' Choice Award, named a TOP PICK author, and been nominated for numerous other awards.

Now living her dream, she resides with her very patient husband and two spoiled cats. When she's not plotting out her next romance, you can find her curled up with a mug of tea and a book. You can learn more about Jennifer at www.JenniferFaye.com

Subscribe to Jennifer's newsletter for news about upcoming releases, bonus content and other special offers.

You can also join her on Twitter, Facebook, or Goodreads.

Also By

Other titles available by Jennifer Faye include:

BLUESTAR ISLAND:

Love Blooms

Harvest Dance

A Lighthouse Café Christmas

Rising Star

Summer by the Beach

Brass Anchor Inn

Summer Refresh

A Seaside Bookshop Christmas

A Lighthouse Snapshot

Inheriting Her Island House

A Mistletoe Kiss

GREEK PARADISE ESCAPE:

Greek Heir to Claim Her Heart

It Started with a Royal Kiss

Second Chance with the Bridesmaid

WEDDING BELLS IN LAKE COMO:

Bound by a Ring & a Secret

Falling for Her Convenient Groom

ONCE UPON A FAIRYTALE:

Beauty & Her Boss

Miss White & the Seventh Heir

Fairytale Christmas with the Millionaire

THE BARTOLINI LEGACY:

The Prince and the Wedding Planner

The CEO, the Puppy & Me

The Italian's Unexpected Heir

GREEK ISLAND BRIDES:

Carrying the Greek Tycoon's Baby

Claiming the Drakos Heir

Wearing the Greek Millionaire's Ring

Click here to find all of Jennifer's titles and buy links.

Made in the USA
Monee, IL
23 June 2026

55567409R00128